Pr
New York Times **and** *USA Today*

Diane Capri

"Full of thrills and tension, but smart and human, too."
Lee Child, #1 New York Times Bestselling Author of Jack
Reacher Thrillers

"[A] welcome surprise….[W]orks from the first page to 'The
End'."
Larry King

"Swift pacing and ongoing suspense are always
present…[L]ikable protagonist who uses her political
connections for a good cause…Readers should eagerly anticipate
the next [book]."
Top Pick, Romantic Times

"…offers tense legal drama with courtroom overtones, twisty
plot, and loads of Florida atmosphere. Recommended."
Library Journal

"[A] fast-paced legal thriller…energetic prose…an appealing
heroine…clever and capable supporting cast…[that will] keep
readers waiting for the next [book]."
Publishers Weekly

"Expertise shines on every page."
Margaret Maron, Edgar, Anthony, Agatha and Macavity Award
Winning MWA Past President

JUSTICE
IS SERVED

by DIANE CAPRI

Justice Is Served: 4 Novellas (Hunt for Justice Series)
Compilation © 2017 Diane Capri, LLC

Cold Justice © 2014 Diane Capri, LLC

False Justice © 2017 Diane Capri, LLC

Fair Justice © 2017 Diane Capri, LLC

True Justice © 2017 Diane Capri, LLC

All Rights Reserved

Published by: AugustBooks
http://www.AugustBooks.com

First Print Edition
ISBN: 978-1-940768-93-9

Original Cover Design: Michelle Priest
Digital Formatting: Author E.M.S.

Published in the United States of America.

Visit the author website:
http://www.DianeCapri.com

BOOKS BY DIANE CAPRI

THE HEIR HUNTER SERIES:
Blood Trails
Trace Evidence

THE HUNT FOR JUSTICE SERIES:
Due Justice (Judge Willa Carson)
Twisted Justice (Judge Willa Carson)
Secret Justice (Judge Willa Carson)
Wasted Justice (Judge Willa Carson)
Raw Justice
Mistaken Justice
Cold Justice (Judge Willa Carson)
False Justice (Judge Willa Carson)
Fair Justice (Judge Willa Carson)
True Justice (Judge Willa Carson)

THE HUNT FOR JACK REACHER SERIES:
Don't Know Jack
Get Back Jack
Jack and Joe
Deep Cover Jack
Jack in a Box
Jack and Kill
Jack in the Green
Jack the Reaper

THE JESS KIMBALL THRILLERS:
Fatal Enemy
Fatal Distraction
Fatal Demand
Fatal Error
Fatal Fall
Fatal Edge
Fatal Game

Dear Friends,

It's an honor and a pleasure to write for you. Like many authors working today, I publish ebooks more frequently than "tree" books. Many of my readers enjoy tree books and also collect them. So when readers asked for a collection of my newest Judge Willa Carson novellas and also asked me to publish them both in print and ebook versions, I was thrilled to oblige.

What I've packaged for you here in *Justice is Served* are four Hunt for Justice Series exciting short reads featuring Judge Willa Carson. I hope you enjoy these collected tales as much as I enjoyed writing them for you.

If you love this collection, please leave a review at the retailer where you bought the book and anywhere else you think readers might see it. Your reviews really help other readers to decide whether or not to give my books a chance.

Now sit back in your easy chair with your favorite beverage close at hand and dive in while I get back to work on more new books especially for you, the best readers in the world. One of these days, I hope to meet you and say thank you in person. Until then—

Caffeinate and Carry On!
Best,

Diane

p.s. I hope you're on my reader group email list, where we let you know about new books, opportunities, contests, giveaways, and, well everything -- first and exclusively. I certainly don't want to leave you out! (And don't worry -- I'll never, ever send you any spam. If it's email from me, you can be sure it's got something terrific to offer.) If you're not signed up and you'd like to be you can do that here: http://dianecapri.com/get-involved/get-my-newsletter/.

CONTENTS

COLD
JUSTICE

*Thank you to some of the best readers in the world:
Lisa Clayton (Marc Clayton), Justin Kemp, and
B.C. Griffin (Jeannine Montgomery) for participating in
our character naming giveaways which make this book a
bit more personal and fun for all of us.*

And for Wilhelmina Boersma, trailblazer extraordinaire.

CAST OF PRIMARY CHARACTERS

Judge Wilhelmina Carson
George Carson

Justin Kemp
Marc Clayton

David Mason
Molly Mason
Leo Richards
Maureen Richards
Randy Trevor
Madeline Trevor

CHAPTER ONE

Traverse City, Michigan

THE DC-9 CIRCLED TRAVERSE City's regional airport,
supplying a panoramic view of the Old Mission Peninsula and
Grand Traverse Bay area that once had been our playground.
Snow covered everything like a cozy comforter and I felt as if
I'd been transported from my ordinary palm trees and sunshine
world to a magical place.

George and I were a little too old, a little too sophisticated,
to be so excited about a winter break. And yet, excited we were.
This was our first vacation in years and I was as thrilled as a
child who discovers her toys from Santa on a snowy Christmas
morning.

We even left our dogs at home, which we almost never did.
Harry and Bess, the lumbering Labradors who shared our life,
would be fine, but we weren't sure we'd survive without them.
We'd never been away from them before. Both of us had a little
separation anxiety already.

Long, empty days stretched before us filled with anticipation

2 | DIANE CAPRI

and the promise of our favorite gifts. Hot chocolate, warm soups. Heavy sweaters, cozy comforters. Blazing fires in the fireplace. Good books. Good booze. Good cigars. No phones. No television.

Even better, no five-star restaurant for George to manage and no federal court justice for me to dispense. For an entire week. Our first real vacation in way too long.

The mere idea of a vacation had carried us through the last few days of hectic preparations and last-minute hearings.

And now, here we were, about to land.

Everything felt absolutely perfect.

Until things started to go wrong.

My self-induced amnesia began to clear. Memories surfaced, reminding me why I left this place a decade ago. For one thing, I remembered I hate the cold.

Unlike a down comforter, the snow blanket on the ground outside promised bone-numbing temps, sending shivers along my entire body. How could I have overlooked that? I wrapped my hands around my biceps and rubbed. Friction, I remembered, produces heat.

Ribbons of twinkling blacktop below nestled between high snowbanks plowed off to each side.

"At least the driving will be clear," George said as he peered across me to look out the window from his seat on the aisle.

He knew I hated treacherous driving in blizzards and black ice because a simple flat tire or fender bender carried the threat of chain reaction collisions and hypothermia.

George was a cold weather enthusiast, so all I said was, "True."

Blacktop roads were the only uncovered ground visible from the plane's window. Picturesque Traverse City nestled on the south side of the bay, which was recognizable only because I knew where the water *should* be. The Great Lakes had frozen to a depth of thirty inches this winter under all that snow, too. Record cold temperatures and snowfall combined to create the mountains of white gold that local ski resorts depended upon for revenue to support them through the lean summer months. Too much of a good thing, I thought, even as it all sparkled in the sharp winter sunlight.

A few minutes later, the captain delivered a perfect touchdown without sliding on the snow-packed runway and the entire cabin of passengers applauded. I'm not a nervous flyer, but the applause made me uneasy. Landing the plane smoothly was a big part of his job. Nobody applauded in my courtroom when I handled my cases especially well. But I imagined they might erupt in riotous celebration if I rarely managed the feat of handling my job.

Still, we'd arrived at our destination. Travel over. Our vacation officially began and I summoned as much of my prior excitement as I could muster.

We disembarked into the frosty jet way. Loaded down with parkas, boots, gloves and carry-ons, we hurried into the over-heated terminal. We made our way like pack animals to claim luggage and collect the rental.

How had I forgotten the sheer burden of moving around in a winter climate?

Half an hour later, with George behind the wheel of the rented Jeep Cherokee sporting a winter wonderland license plate and me trying to read the yellow highlighted route on the map because GPS was unreliable here, we traveled along the blacktop, skimming through the seven-foot snow tunnel open to the sky and the breathtaking beauty captured me once again.

Or maybe it was the frigid and unrelenting cold that stole my breath away.

Eventually, we reached U.S. 31 North, left Traverse City behind and headed toward Pleasant Harbor, about fifty miles north on the two-lane, according to the map.

We should have been there in about an hour. Ninety minutes tops.

CHAPTER TWO

THE ROAD HUGGED EAST Bay all the way up. The driving was easy. The day was gorgeous. *What's not to like?* I chided myself.

On our left was an unobstructed vista across frozen Grand Traverse Bay toward Old Mission Peninsula. Grape fields and cherry orchards barely poked above the snow. Shanties perched on the ice for fishing and there were a couple of ice boats, sails filled with blasting cold wind, racing back and forth. A recent storm had dipped even the smallest tree branches in ice gloves that sparkled in the sunlight.

We both wore our sunglasses, which seemed silly when the temperature here was exactly one hundred degrees lower than what we'd left at home this morning. According to the Jeep's thermometer, it was a frosty three degrees outside. Yet the sun's glare was brighter than back in Tampa.

Snow was piled five feet high on the right side of the road, exposing a view of nothing but a solid white wall outside the passenger window.

I reached over and flipped the fan to maximum and

simultaneously pressed the button to lower the window.

George asked, more than a little testily, "I like the cold, but are you trying to freeze me to death?"

"Listening to the quiet," I told him.

The snow covered everything with a blanket of silence that muffled even the country sounds of the farmland we were driving through now. Except for what could have been snowmobiles in the distance, I didn't hear a cow or a horse or anything. Blissful silence.

"Well, can you just imagine the quiet?" George snapped. "I'm freezing my ass off over here."

I would have refused on principle alone, but it was really quite cold. I rolled the window back up, preparing to give him some lip about it, when we rounded a curve in the road and I glanced out the windshield.

"George! Stop!" I yelled and braced for impact.

He slammed on the brakes, both hands on the wheel. A sound like "Yaaaaaa!" exploded from his throat as he pumped the brake pedal.

Something oddly detached in my mind wondered whether pumping the brakes was the right thing to do.

The Jeep slewed into the oncoming traffic lane. George wrestled with the steering wheel and got back on track, but we continued to slide. Finally, the Jeep stopped.

Mere inches before we'd have slammed into the rear of the white Toyota SUV sitting dead still in the middle of our northbound traffic lane.

If we hadn't been wearing our seatbelts, we'd both have been thrown into the windshield. As it was, we were jerked back like snapped rubber bands. Fortunately, the airbags didn't deploy, although I wondered why not while my heart pounded like a thundering herd of wild buffalo in my chest and the sound amplified in my ears.

A few moments of silence enveloped the Jeep inside and out as we gathered our senses and discovered that we were not hurt.

The fluffy down parka I wore over a heavy wool sweater padded me enough that I might avoid a dandy seatbelt-shaped bruise across my torso tomorrow.

Otherwise, we were shook up, but fine.

"What the hell?" George eventually asked. His tone implied actual curiosity, a bit of his trademark composure returning. "There's not a sign of a taillight or a flasher on that vehicle."

The Toyota hadn't moved since I'd first glimpsed it. I could see no brake nor tail lights nor flashers of any kind, either.

And the engine was off.

If there had been snow on the road, the white Toyota would have been all but invisible. As it was, the blacktop beneath its wheels had provided enough contrast for me to see it. Thank God.

George flipped on the Jeep's flashers and unbuckled his seatbelt.

"Where are you going?" I asked him, still checking to be sure I hadn't broken any bones, trying to calm my heartbeat which was still pounding "Wipeout" in my head.

Without answering, he opened the door and stepped out onto the center of the road. "George?"

"I'll be right back. The driver may be in trouble here," he said, in what turned out to be the understatement of the century.

CHAPTER THREE

WE HADN'T SEEN ANOTHER vehicle for a while, and leaving the Jeep in the middle of the travel lane didn't seem wise. The snow wall on the right shoulder left us no choice. If another vehicle slammed into the Jeep, I didn't want to be sitting inside it. Time to get out while I still could.

After a couple of tries, I realized we were so close to the snow wall on the right that I couldn't open the passenger door wide enough to exit. *Swell.*

I wiggled around and lifted one long leg and ridiculously huge boot over the console in the middle of the Jeep's front seat, straddling the gearshift for a few moments before I managed to get the other leg over.

There are plenty of times when being almost six feet tall is a real handicap. Climbing around inside of vehicles while dressed like a Laplander was one of them.

Eventually, I managed to get myself out through the driver's side door and joined George where he was standing, stock still, at the Toyota. His gaze focused straight ahead.

The first thing I noticed was the driver.

A man. Thirty-five, maybe forty. Impossible to guess his height or weight because of his position and attire. He was dressed in heavy winter gear like we were, except his hands were bare of gloves and very pink with cold.

His head was bowed and he slumped forward slightly, held in place by his seat belt. Maybe he'd had a heart attack or a stroke or something. Maybe he would be okay.

Why wasn't George trying to get into the car and help the guy?

My gaze rested on the Toyota's windows and I recognized the whole problem.

Involuntarily, my breath sucked in with a vacuum-like roar in the silence.

The driver's side window was shattered but still in place. The passenger side window was blown out, but a few shards remained, covered with blood and flesh and bone. And gray matter that could only have been the driver's brain. Some of the smaller grisly bits had already frosted over in icy crystals. The rest was probably embedded in the snow bank opposite where we stood.

My joy in this magic world had shattered, too, just like the glass on the Toyota's windows. Nerves hummed along my body unrelated to the frigid cold. Warnings I didn't heed.

The scene was surreal. A murder in the middle of nowhere, nobody around, the Toyota and its occupant blending with the pure sparkling snow but sticking out, too. Unmistakably murder.

The area felt sinister to me now, menacing. I looked around for the shooter, even as I knew he was probably long gone. If he were nearby, watching, he'd wear camouflage to make him invisible. Either way, I didn't see him. Which made things worse instead of better.

I'd seen gunshot wounds to the head that weren't fatal, but I could tell even from a distance that this wasn't one of them. Still, to be sure, I opened the door, pulled off my glove, reached through and touched his cold and bright pink flesh above his carotid artery to confirm.

He felt frozen, almost, which made me wonder how long he'd been sitting here, dead or alive. The interior of the Toyota smelled like blood and frost. Or maybe my imagination conjured those odors because as cold as he was, the smells should have already dissipated.

I stepped back and re-gloved. The temperature was way too cold for unprotected flesh to be exposed very long without frostbite.

"Do you have your cell phone?" George asked me, his question grabbing my gaze from the evidence spatter.

In all our lives together, the more serious the situation, the calmer George got. It's one of the things that drives me crazy about him. Another man would have been shouting, panicked. In other words, normal. But not George.

"I do," I replied.

"Call the police," was all he said, as if the call would solve everything. Which, of course, it would not. No one knew better than me that discovering a murder victim led to years of pain for everyone involved.

But we couldn't simply leave the scene for someone else to discover, either.

So I pulled out my cell and made the call while I continued to scan for shooters.

CHAPTER FOUR

I MARCHED IN PLACE, trying to keep warm, which was impossible. Deep breaths drawn in through my nose burned all the way down into my lungs. Sunlight glared off the snow, blinding, even through my reflective sunglasses. Cold-induced tears seeped from the corners of my eyes and trailed warmth down my cheeks, lasting only a moment before all warmth evaporated with the saline.

George had crossed the two-lane road and was now examining snowmobile tracks on the side nearest the shoreline, opposite our two vehicles. No clue what he hoped to find over there, but I didn't feel like tromping around and didn't discourage his explorations beyond reminding him to be careful of the evidence.

We could have collected the victim and driven him back to town, but there seemed to be little point to that option, and it would have been counterproductive. Crime scene techs should sort this one out fairly quickly. As long as we could avoid a chain-reaction collision until help arrived.

The 911 operator had assured me that responders were on

their way. The first to arrive would probably be from the Michigan State police post in Traverse City, she'd said. When I asked her how long it would take, she'd deflected. I looked at my watch. Only ten minutes had passed since the call and we were about an hour from town. I guessed we probably had fifty minutes of time to kill.

We remained alone with the body, the cold and the now-screaming quiet.

Seeking something useful to do that wouldn't destroy the crime scene, something mundane that would make the scene less real while it kept my circulation going, I looked in the back of the Jeep and found four small plastic orange cones and flares in the emergency kit.

I walked back from the Jeep to the curve in the road that blocked a traveler's view of both vehicles and put two cones in the northbound lane. Then, I walked the other two up to the southbound lane, about 100 feet in front of the Toyota. The cones might not have made us any safer, but I felt better doing something. Warmer, too.

When I returned to the Jeep, George had finished his survey of the snowmobile tracks and the rest of the accident scene.

"It looks like a rifle shot," he said, pointing to the shattered driver-side glass.

"Deer hunters live in this area and just about everyone knows how to shoot a shotgun," I replied. "But this looks like above-average marksmanship to me."

George was a handgun enthusiast. But I knew more about forensic evidence in firearm-related deaths than he did. Besides my personal experience at crime scenes, I'd also heard plenty of expert testimony on the subject.

JUSTICE IS SERVED | 15

"You think the killer shot at the car while it was moving?" he asked.

The possibility didn't seem likely to me. Any kind of drive-by shootings were fairly rare in Tampa, but out here they had to be non-existent. Even a highly-trained military sniper preferred not to aim at a random moving target, given a choice.

"Doubtful. Come on. Let me show you something," I replied.

George followed me up the road a little way and around the bend where I pointed to the snow covered pavement in front of the Toyota closer than the spot where I'd placed the orange cones.

"The wind has been gusting hard. Might have blown the snow over the road there," George said.

The road had been plowed clean. At some point yesterday or the day before the sun had heated the blacktop enough to melt any snow that had been left after the plow came through. We'd been lucky enough to drive on good road. Which was one of the reasons we hadn't slammed into the Toyota. The pavement was fairly dry and mostly clear.

Everywhere along the blacktop, that is, except the one spot.

"Look at this." George walked near the shoulder a little farther north. I followed him. He showed me where tracks indicated a snowmobile had left the snow and pulled onto the dry road, dragging some of the snow that had been on its runners along with it and transferring that snow onto the blacktop.

George said, "The snowmobile pulled up here and blocked the traveled lane of the highway." He gestured with his gloved hand.

"But the Toyota never got this far," I replied.

"So you think the snowmobile rider walked back and flagged

the Toyota down?" George asked me, as if I had a crystal ball.

"That doesn't explain the broken driver-side window and the long-range rifle shot," I said. I stood where the snowmobile must have been parked and looked south toward the Toyota. "You can't see the vehicle from here because of the bend in the road and the amount of snow piled up and because it's white. If it had been a dark color, maybe it would have stood out."

I looked at George to see if he understood my meaning. He nodded, but I explained anyway, to be sure. "Not just a lucky shot by some guy taking target practice as the cars went by. The snowmobiler stopped the Toyota intentionally."

This was more bone chilling than the frigid cold air surrounding us, but I waited for him to recognize and verbalize the only possible conclusion. He got it fairly quickly.

CHAPTER FIVE

"WHICH MEANS THE SNOWMOBILER knew who was driving the car and wanted to kill him," he said slowly.

Hearing it from him didn't make the truth any better.

"It looks like a set up. Yes," I said.

I looked around again. Unlikely the guy would still be anywhere within fifty miles of us. But I didn't like standing out in the open like this.

George bent his knees and lowered his body so that his gaze was even with what must have been the snowmobiler's sightline. Then he stood and walked over to the snowmobile tracks on the other side of the road again.

"Let's not disturb the scene any more than we have already," I told him, knowing only too well the number of problems a contaminated crime scene would present at the killer's eventual trial. And there would be a trial if I had anything to say about it.

Glancing at my watch again, I saw that only twenty minutes had passed since we'd first found the Toyota. I was thoroughly chilled outside by the weather and inside by the cold-blooded murder. Maybe the shock of the entire thing was starting to settle into my bones a little, too.

Without thinking, I took a deep breath and the cold seared all the way into my lungs again. A hint of pine scented the air and added to the burn.

George returned to the area where I'd found the snow on the road and looked at it more closely, squatting down to get a better angle. A stronger breeze had kicked up. Clouds of dry snow swirled fine white powder around us now, chafing my face and forcing my hands deeper into my pockets. One of my gloved hands connected with my phone.

Which reminded me that I should take some photos of the scene before the weather destroyed even more evidence. I removed my gloves to operate the camera and my fingers immediately stiffened as if my warm blood had immediately chilled to pudding.

The brittle cold had sucked humidity from the air and the snow. Snowmobile tracks on the road itself, if any had been there before we arrived, were blown away. By the time the state police arrived, the tracks would be completely gone, as if they'd never existed at all. No doubt the killer was counting on that very thing.

I grabbed as many snapshots as I could, blowing on my fingers from time to time to keep the joints flexible. Documenting the crime scene as well as possible under the circumstances.

George began to walk slowly back toward the Toyota until he reached it, then turned and walked forward again. I tagged along, partly documenting everything with the photos and a few minutes of video, and partly to keep warm. It wasn't until we were at the bend in the road ahead that he stopped again.

"What's bothering you?" I asked.

"From here, I can see the Toyota. But I wouldn't have been able to put that shot through the side window. The angle's wrong," he told me. George has won several marksmanship prizes over the years. If he couldn't have made the shot, it probably couldn't be done. At least, not by a recreational deer hunter.

The implication in his words coiled my stomach into knots. I pulled the parka's hood over my head, re-gloved and stuffed my hands deep into my pockets to warm up. And to stop the shaking.

I looked around. The crispness now present in the air further sharpened my awareness. "The snowmobile driver had an accomplice. Two people who wanted this guy dead instead of only one."

We remained easy targets, standing out here, I thought again as I looked around once more, but saw nothing unusual that I hadn't noted before.

"Maybe." George continued walking toward the car, looking around on the ground. A fine powder of white snow now dusted wide swaths of the road, while in other spots, the black asphalt was clear. No particular pattern revealed itself. The wind whipped the snow now in gusts that stayed only moments and then blew away.

George was looking down, walking slowly, one foot in front of the other. I walked behind him, looking backward, still concerned that another car might come along and slam into us, or the shooter might lay in wait, or a thousand other things could happen.

You never see the bullet that gets you.

We saw no one. The wide red line on the map suggested this was a busy road, but we had not seen another car for almost thirty minutes. Maybe the shooter had known the area well. Maybe he'd known the roadway would be deserted. Made sense as a working hypothesis, at least.

My teeth had started to chatter and my nose was running, too. Dying from exposure wasn't what I'd had planned for our vacation. And I was feeling so cold now that I began to wonder how long it would take me, a thirty-nine-year-old woman, five feet eleven inches tall, warmly dressed, to succumb.

But then I saw something I'd missed.

"Willa, let's wait in the Jeep. I'm freezing," George said, before he began walking in that direction. He'd apparently satisfied his curiosity. For now.

I barely heard him.

About five feet in front of the Toyota, I bent down and stared at the ground.

"What is it?" George asked, a little irritably, when he walked over to join me.

I pointed with a gloved hand to a couple of marks in the snow, very faint. "Doesn't that look like something heavy was placed there and then removed?"

He looked at the snow where I'd pointed. "Maybe. Like what?" George looked back at the Toyota. Almost immediately, he saw what I'd seen.

The Toyota's right front tire was flat.

"Maybe a board or something with a sharp spike in it. It's hard to say. But it worked effectively to stop the Toyota," I replied.

We hadn't noticed the flat tire before because we'd been walking along the left side, away from the snow wall on the right shoulder of the road.

It took George a few long seconds to realize what the flat tire meant. When he figured it out without any further comment from me, the knots in my stomach pulled tighter and I began to shiver so much that when George stood up and turned to face me, he actually noticed.

"Here. You're freezing," he said, wrapping me in a big hug for body warmth.

Before we could say anything more, the promised Michigan State Police trooper pulled to a stop behind the Jeep.

I don't think I'd ever been so glad to see a cop in my life.

CHAPTER SIX

EXACTLY FIFTY-TWO MINUTES AFTER we had called, the
state trooper arrived in an old-fashioned navy-blue patrol car
with a single red flashing gumball on the top. Must have stopped
for donuts.

Thank God the driver of the car was beyond help when we'd
made the call or he'd have died waiting.

The trooper approached and we introduced ourselves. "I'm
Trooper Justin Kemp," he said, handing George a business card.
It was hard to see what he looked like in the blinding sunlight,
through my sunglasses, while he wore that big brimmed hat and
sunglasses. He seemed friendly enough, though.

I pulled out my cell and snapped a couple of pictures of the
flat tire while George told Kemp what happened and what we'd
concluded from our preliminary investigation.

"Mrs. Carson, Mr. Carson," Trooper Kemp said as he
tipped his old-fashioned hat with the flat, wide brim that
shadowed his features more than it should have. "Please
don't take this the wrong way. I mean you no disrespect. But
we will conduct our own investigation and analyze our own

evidence and come to the conclusions the evidence supports."

His attitude got my back up, so I said, "There's no question about it. There were at least two people involved. And it was a set up. For sure. While we're standing here, the killers are either getting away or taking aim. Which do you think it is?"

He replied, "There's a blizzard on the way according to the weather reports. The forecast says we'll be walloped with four to five feet of drifting snow before this one passes through. Teams are on the way here now and we need to get this crime scene cleared while we still can."

George and I had dealt with police officers many times before. They generally felt they were better at doing their jobs than we were. Sometimes, they were right.

Sometimes, not so much.

Today, I was more than glad to leave the young trooper to his work. He was right that the evidence had already begun to deteriorate and a blizzard would make processing the scene impossible. I was cold, and tired, and I didn't want to stand around out here and argue. I wanted a warm bath and a stiff drink.

Not necessarily in that order.

When we didn't protest, Trooper Kemp said, "I do need to take a tape-recorded statement from you and then I'll let you go on your way."

"We'll do the recorded statement later, when you're finished here. We have some questions for you, too." I reached into my pocket and pulled out one of my official business cards with the raised gold seal issued by the United States government to all Federal District Court judges. "My cell phone number is on the back. We'll be staying with Marc Clayton, in Pleasant Harbor. You know him, don't you?"

"It's a small community, ma'am. Everybody knows everybody here."

He took my card and glanced down to read it and the hat brim completely covered his face. When he looked up, he raised his hand to tip the brim again, slightly more respect in his tone this time when he said, "I'll stop by this afternoon if weather permits, Judge Carson."

"Or we'll call you," I promised.

I hooked my arm through George's and led him toward the Jeep. The trooper walked with us as if he planned to make sure we went on our way. While I struggled to maneuver myself over the console and into the passenger seat again, George asked, "So you knew the victim, then?"

Trooper Kemp seemed to be about the same age as the man in the car, maybe thirty-five, maybe a year or five either side. If they were both local, they'd have known each other. He probably shouldn't have answered, but he must have realized a judge could be trusted and we could hang around all day if he didn't.

Kemp said, "His name is Leo Richards. He owns the hardware store in Pleasant Harbor. He's married to Maureen and he has a little girl." As George moved toward his seat, Kemp added unnecessarily, "I'd appreciate it if you wouldn't say anything about this until we get a chance to notify the family."

"We don't envy you that job," George told him as he settled into the driver's seat. He turned the ignition on and the heater to full blast. Maybe the car would warm up again so that we could both thaw out someday.

We snugged our seat belts a little bit tighter this time and George carefully pulled out and around the Toyota. My desire to take pictures of the snow had evaporated, which was good because the phone's battery was low and I didn't want to run it out completely in case we needed to make another call. The phone charger was packed in one of the suitcases. I could charge up once we reached the cottage.

As we drove north, away from the scene, I glanced into the side mirror. Kemp stood, holding a cell phone to his ear, watching us go, maybe calling in our license plate or something. Two vehicles with flashing lights pulled up behind him. Probably part of his team. When we rounded the first curve, I lost sight of Kemp, but I still wondered who he'd been talking to.

There was no rush to take my statement. I wouldn't forget anything about the man with the pink hands and the hole in his head and his brains splashed all over the inside of his frosty vehicle. No chance of that. No chance I'd let this murder remain unsolved, either. It might not be my jurisdiction, but justice is always my job and I liked it that way. Judges are like cops. We're never off duty.

"You sure know how to start a vacation," I said, once my teeth stopped chattering, already thinking about the next steps.

CHAPTER SEVEN

WE CONTINUED ON OUR way toward Pleasant Harbor in silence. The clean snow had lost its appeal and clouds had moved in to replace the sparkling sunlight just as our vacation's luster had dulled. We traveled with our separate thoughts for companionship, until a small sign on the right hand side of the road caught my attention.

"Welcome to Pleasant Harbor. Population 1,202," I read aloud simply to break the silence. *Now only 1,201.*

The first flakes of the promised blizzard began to fall. George flipped the windshield wipers on and stopped at the traffic light.

Smoke rose from the buildings to our left where U.S. 31 abutted Michigan Highway M-244. Once again, the area seemed deserted. In the summer, a line of traffic stopped here and then filed off in all directions. Not today. The hardy residents were probably huddled inside by their fireplaces, which was where I'd hoped to be by now.

Many times we'd turned right at this intersection to continue on toward Mackinaw City and then to romantic getaways on

Mackinac Island. But today, we'd turn left to downtown Pleasant Harbor.

The light turned green and we travelled a bit farther into town before George said, "Looks pretty much the same as the last time we were here, don't you think?"

"It's hard to tell with the snow covering everything, but I don't see very many new buildings, if that's what you mean." I wanted conversation, but discussing the town or the weather seemed so banal now. I didn't feel like socializing. My thoughts continued to return to the murder as if a video loop replayed in my head. There was something else about it that was odd, but what was it?

"What if we take a short ride through town and head to Eagle Creek Cafe? It's late, but we might still get lunch." I didn't say anything. "Or we could go directly to the cottage now, if you'd rather get unpacked." More silence. "Willa?" He took his right hand off the steering wheel, where it had been firmly planted since we'd returned to the Jeep, and placed it over mine in my lap. His gloved fingers intertwined with mine.

I said, "I've seen murder victims before. I just didn't expect to find a gruesome one this afternoon."

"I know."

"The landscape looked soothing, so pristine and beautiful."

"I know."

"A man murdered in a tiny, peaceful hamlet shakes your faith." That was my problem. I kept forgetting that the gun lobby is right about some things. It is people who kill people. Environment didn't change basic human nature.

"Confining humans in a small space as harsh as this one and expecting them to peacefully coexist is probably too much to ask for." George squeezed my fingers a little tighter to signal that he needed his hand back. I let him go and felt immediately bereft.

Snow was falling faster now. He increased the wiper speed.

Something more about the crime scene still niggled at the back of my brain. But it disappeared around the corners whenever I almost grasped it. The best thing was to treat it like a timid kitten and wait until it came far enough into the open to seize it.

George had turned the Jeep onto Main Street. "Let's get some lunch. We can meet up with Marc and maybe find something else to talk about for a while," he said.

"You just want to get to Marc and talk shop, don't you? Have you forgotten you're on vacation?"

He laughed and said, "Have you forgotten you're on vacation, too?"

"Fair point." After that, I sat with my thoughts.

We traveled over the drawbridge on the west end of Main Street, which was perpetually down in the winter since the river froze and no boats could pass through anyway. The snow had been plowed from the grates of the bridge and the Jeep's tires chirruped as we passed over.

George turned right and traveled along the winding street that followed the shoreline, the frozen edge of Lake Michigan stilled now in ice hard enough to drive snowmobiles across. On the left side of the street sat stately nineteenth-century mansions from a bygone era when the town was ruled by lumber barons.

Nothing much seemed different, though.

Back when George and I were Detroit residents, we visited Pleasant Harbor often. It was a lovely resort town, summer and winter, back then. The deep, cold lake was beautiful in a way completely different from the Gulf of Mexico that surrounds our home in Tampa. Golf resorts and ski resorts and wineries and outdoor activities abounded nearby. Although the population triples with tourists who bring along their Grosse Pointe and Birmingham and Chicago suburban money as well as their big city values, I'd never felt threatened or vulnerable to violence here.

Had the town changed that much since we'd moved south?

True, only those sturdy souls who can survive over 200 inches of snow and subzero temperatures with high levels of humidity, exist here full time. Theirs wasn't a lifestyle for the faint of heart. Meaning it wasn't a place where George and I chose to survive. We'd known that back when we lived here and we knew it now.

I considered what George had said about the harsh winter conditions these folks lived in. Maybe, if you were forced to stay here year round, it was like a prison. A beautiful frozen prison, sure. But still a prison. Perhaps cabin fever set in too easily and led to depraved inmate behavior. Seems I read something about cannibals in Wisconsin once.

Which wasn't an excuse for murder. Never had been. Never would be. We prosecute those who kill in prison, too.

The curious thing was how pink Richards' body was. I'd seen it before in autopsy photographs of carbon monoxide victims. But this guy hadn't died from any kind of poisoning, obviously.

The more I concentrated, the less I understood, so I let it go. Temporarily.

CHAPTER EIGHT

WE CROSSED OVER INTO what had once been no-man's land and was now, perhaps, some of the most desirable real estate in Pleasant Harbor.

Milliken Boulevard was a picturesque four-lane that had once divided the town in half, separating the regular citizens on the east side from those confined in the asylum on the west side. A train ran between them alongside the boulevard for good measure.

"Would you have lived there?" George asked, pointing toward the castle-like estate ahead.

The former Eagle Creek State Hospital had once been another type of prison. A jewel in the crown of medicine so bright it had boasted a two-year waiting list for new patients. I believed the waiting list had resulted back then partly because conditions in the asylum were better in many ways.

"I'd have tried," I said, only too happy to embrace the distracting change of subject.

"Why?"

"The hospital was fully equipped with electricity long before the town. That alone would have enticed me to enter."

"Because?"

I was a constant reader and he always teased me about it.

"Light to read by at night instead of an oil lamp or a candle."

He laughed. "But surely that's not all?"

"Two more things."

"Which are?"

"Remember I took that tour of the place when we were here last time? Did you know it had two sets of underground tunnels, one for its sophisticated steam heating system and another for moving people that connected the buildings? Thus," I raised my index finger, "heat without hassle. I wouldn't have had to chop wood or haul coal. And," I raised my second finger, "asylum residents never needed to venture outside in the damn frozen tundra. That sounds like heaven right about now."

We'd entered the grounds. Various buildings were spread over several acres of what was probably lawn under all that snow.

"This place is amazing and beautiful and awful and creepy all at the same time, isn't it?" George asked.

It was.

Through sixty years of its history, the grand old buildings served as an asylum for patients with communicable diseases, mental disorders and, it was said, a place to imprison uncontrollable menopausal women.

As treatments and vaccines and pharmacology improved, budgets dwindled until the facility eventually closed. That was long before we moved to Tampa. Over the decades, some of the buildings had been condemned and demolished. Restoration of the others had to have been a nightmare.

"What happened to the patients, I wonder?" George asked.

"Our tour guide said there weren't many left at the end. The last few were simply released. They literally opened the doors and let them walk away. Which increased the local homeless population exponentially," I replied.

Could one of them have murdered Leo Richards? I quickly shook my head as soon as the idea surfaced. The murder was too well planned and executed to have been the work of a mental patient.

These days, the entire Eagle Creek Village complex had been reborn into a multi-use historical district filled with specialty boutiques, offices, condominiums, apartments, an inn, and restaurants. Some things hadn't changed much, though. Eagle Creek Village also boasted a two-year waiting list as its predecessor had.

"They're doing a masterful job with the restoration," he said.

George turned left down a two-lane driveway that opened onto a flat gravel lot. He parked the Jeep near the front door of what had once been the sprawling main building of the hospital and was now called Eagle Creek Village Center. This was where our friend Marc had relocated his Cafe.

There was no sign out front. For many years the only five-star restaurant in Northern Michigan, Marc's tony eatery didn't need a sign to advertise its presence to potential diners. Word of mouth had kept the restaurant full to overflowing when it had been located a few miles south of town. Now that it was housed in prestige and surrounded by history, reservations stacked up like magic.

George turned off the Jeep and looked toward me. "Let's not talk about the murder to Marc. I'm sure he'll find out soon enough."

"Works for me."

Trooper Kemp would be calling this afternoon. More

statements would be required after that, maybe testimony at some point. The process would be endless, even if the locals were up to the challenge of apprehending the killer. If that didn't happen quickly, then I'd become more involved than I already was. A quiet hour or two before the next episode seemed like a great idea.

George took my hand and squeezed it. "Come on, Mighty Mouse. I'll buy you lunch. Fortify you for crime fighting later."

He jumped out before I could hit him with a snappy comeback.

CHAPTER NINE

GEORGE CAME AROUND TO open my door and I left the warmth of the Jeep's interior for the unrelenting cold. Snow was falling heavily.

Under the snow, Eagle Creek's grounds were beautifully landscaped with wild English gardens. The lawns were dotted with tables and chairs under tents around a large lily-pond for alfresco dining. One of the old buildings had been demolished and its foundation converted into a bocce court. George and I had spent many idyllic evenings engaged in just such pursuits.

None of that was visible now.

It was March second. In three weeks, the calendar would declare spring. In Pleasant Harbor, Mother Nature would ignore the declaration for at least eight weeks. I remembered one Fourth of July when the temperature only reached forty-four degrees and the crazy ones in our group had insisted on swimming anyway. The memory alone made my teeth chatter.

The parking lot had been plowed to pack down the snow, but bits of gravel showed through here and there. Snow piles higher than my head outlined the edges of the lot. Several other vehicles, including a few snowmobiles, were parked and snow dusted, suggesting they'd been there a while. The entire grounds, except the entryway to the main building, were covered by even more snow.

"Let's get inside," George said, as he pulled his parka hood to cover his head and took my arm. I raised my hood and followed along, head down. We slid along the length of the plowed sidewalk, trudged up the stairs to the front door and stepped into a warm and inviting piece of history.

We waited at the hostess stand because the Cafe's main dining room was busier than we'd expected. Restaurants are usually quiet at three o'clock in the afternoon and the chef is busy with preparations for dinner. But Eagle Creek Cafe buzzed with conversation.

A couple of minutes later, the hostess returned to seat us. "Are you folks joining the bridge club? Mrs. Trevor didn't tell me she expected more members. You're a bit late and we've already closed the buffet, but we can find you a table in the back if that's okay and we'd be happy to serve you something from the menu."

"We're not with the club. Simply here for one of your amazing meals, please," George replied.

She collected the menus and, a little relieved, said, "Certainly. Right this way."

We were led to a table close to the kitchen and near an exit door, past several full tables of bridge players and a couple of lingering groups who seemed to be finished but reluctant to leave the warmth inside for the blizzard outdoors. Or maybe they weren't aware of the blizzard because the Cafe was located in what had once been the basement of the building. The windows were small and square and high on the walls. Seated diners would have to look above their heads to notice the storm and they were more focused on their meals and bridge games.

"I'm sorry that this is our last table. But the bridge club has filled the restaurant to capacity. Usually they're gone by now, but Mrs. Richards said it was tournament day or something like that," she said.

Mrs. Richards? The name hit me like a quick Taser hit.

George, ever the gallant restaurateur, replied, "This will be fine. The food will be marvelous no matter where we're served, I'm sure."

"Thank you for understanding," she said, leaving our menus and dashing off to a table of four women, three of whom looked enough alike to be sisters, and a fourth who seemed to be annoyed at their lack of concentration.

George grinned. "The dreaded Mrs. Trevor calls, I presume."

"Maybe," I said, quietly. "But is Mrs. Richards the victim's wife?"

"In a town this small, she's got to be a relative, at least."

Once upon a time, the cafe's kitchen was the site of the hospital morgue. Not an appetizing factoid right at the moment, to be sure, so I didn't mention it to George. Instead, we talked about this and that, avoiding the subject of our grisly discovery until after our food was presented.

One thing about a gourmet restaurant, it's usually stocked with fabulous ingredients for all sorts of wonderful food. Even if a guest arrives in the middle of the afternoon, on a weekday, in the middle of a blizzard, they won't go hungry.

We ordered Gouda cheese omelets with fresh chives, toast with butter and locally made tart cherry jam, and a stainless carafe filled with nectar of the gods. Until the coffee aroma wafted to my nose, I hadn't realized I was so hungry.

George fell in like a man who hadn't eaten in a year. I picked up my pace.

The conversation noise level in the room and our isolation near the kitchen and the exit presented an opportunity for a private discussion. There was only one subject on my mind.

"Premeditated murder, obviously," I said. I willed him to test my conclusions aloud, hoping I'd made an error or missed something important.

He nodded between mouthfuls.

"I'm thinking the right handgun from the proper distance would produce those results," I said. "It looked like a rifle shot, but sometimes it's hard to tell for sure before the forensics are completed."

These had to be the best eggs ever. I actually hate eggs, so maybe they tasted great because I hadn't eaten anything at all today and my stomach had been tied in knots since I'd first seen the Toyota. The cheese probably had something to do with it, too.

I finished my thought process to get us on the same wavelength. "The killer put something in the road to stop the car with a flat tire. He's close to the car and the victim. He wouldn't have remounted the snowmobile, returned to the field, aimed and fired a rifle to cause the effects we saw at the scene. That would take time and be a huge hassle and someone could easily have come along to witness everything. None of that is reasonable. A handgun is a better answer."

"Makes sense," he said. He warmed up his coffee from the carafe and poured more for me. "Unless the victim was the unlucky lotto winner of a random shooting."

"Then why not just shoot as the vehicles passed by and hope to get lucky instead of setting up a flat tire to stop one?"

"And the accomplice?" he asked.

"There to help make the job go faster, probably. Or maybe they were worried the driver would put up a fight and they'd need two people to subdue him. We won't know what their thinking was unless we find them and they tell us," I said.

"So someone who knew the victim knew he would be traveling that road this morning. The killers laid in wait to execute him," George said. "Is that about it?"

This was the only reasonable conclusion and I'd reached it an hour ago. But I'd wanted another answer and after a while, I'd found one.

George piled tart cherry jam on the toast before taking another bite.

"Actually, I think it's worse than that," I said.

There certainly were worse ways to die than being shot in the head. I had presided over countless criminal trials and accepted dozens of guilty pleas. Killers admitted variously depraved murders for both logical and insane reasons. I refused to organize killers into classes, some better and some worse. Killing another human being was crossing a Rubicon to me. Justice for that should always be swift and sure.

It was the intellectual aspect of the murder that had captured George's imagination, though. He was a good strategist. One of the best. He enjoyed figuring out both the good and bad puzzles in life. So I waited to see if his conclusion was the same as mine.

Finally, he said it. "The killer arranged for the victim to be in that place at that time."

My breath snagged. I'd wanted to be wrong. An orchestrated execution with a high level of premeditation. A smart killer, a planner. Someone who deliberately intended to end a human life and get away with murder. Someone who knew how to make that happen.

If killers were classified by degree of guilt, and that is how our legal system operates, then the cold-blooded executioner was the most heinous. What could a Pleasant Harbor hardware store owner with a wife and young daughter have done to inspire such malice? Sometimes, the depravity of my fellow humans made me want to hide in a hole like a groundhog, never to come out, even to predict the spring.

George continued talking almost to himself now, trying to work it out. "Predictability was required. What makes the most sense to me is the killer called Richards on a cell phone and told him something that caused him to travel that road at just the right time."

The eggs didn't seem so tasty any more, and I pushed my plate away. "But the victim lived here. His car was traveling *toward* Pleasant Harbor, not away from it. How do you explain that?"

"I can't explain it, except to say that the killer must have known Richards' plans for the day or somehow participated in them." George finished his coffee, ate the rest of his toast and jam. The conversation didn't seem to be affecting his appetite at all.

My coffee was cold and the omelet congealed, half eaten and unappetizing now.

Eventually, he pushed his empty plate aside. "You may not get more food for a while," George told me in the same way a mother might scold a child.

"I guess I'll have to take my chances," I replied.

George refilled his coffee, offered me a fresh cup. I shook

my head and pulled my parka over my shoulders. "We probably saw him out there. You realize that, right?"

We'd seen snowmobilers skimming along the edge of the lake on the way into town north of the crime scene. At the time, I'd thought the riders were lucky to be enjoying fresh trails. After we found the Toyota's flat tire, a more sinister image intruded.

As if conjured by our conversation, I heard the unmistakable sound of a snowmobile pulling up out front. At first, I thought I was imagining it, but when the engine died, profound silence reinforced the prior noise.

I looked toward the exit door. Stomping on the porch, probably the rider knocking snow off his boots. The level of tension in my body had escalated to the point where I almost jumped up to hide. As ridiculous as it seemed, it somehow felt possible that a killer was about to enter the room.

George made no move to rise, but he must have sensed something. As he had back when we were in the car, he reached over and placed his hand on top of mine. This time, the gesture didn't reassure.

CHAPTER TEN

THE BACK DOOR OPENED and an Eskimo powered through. A huge man, maybe three hundred pounds, wrapped from head to toe in navy blue down-filled Gortex. His face was covered by a black ski mask that revealed only his eyes, nose and mouth. Steam radiated off him. Oversized boots and gloves made his feet and hands look the size of tennis rackets. He stomped his boots to knock the last of the snow off onto the mat.

When he pushed the fur-trimmed hood of his parka away from his head and yanked off the ski-mask, his face looked reddened by the cold. White skin with a few freckles. Brown hair, brown eyes, bushy brows. Totally ordinary. Which didn't mean he was innocent.

Witness after witness who testified in my courtroom describing a killer usually said, "He looked so normal." Or, "He was such a nice man."

Sure he was nice and normal, until he deliberately caused a blowout of one of your tires and then executed you with a single bullet to the head.

Could this guy have been today's shooter?

"Hello, folks!" he said to us, in a rather jovial way for a cold-blooded killer. "I see the bridge club is still at it. Those women have some stamina, don't they?"

He huffed and puffed with the effort of removing his snowmobile suit over the girth of his stomach. As he hung each piece of gear in a closet by the door, he kept talking. "I'm David Mason, one of the chefs here. I ran out of butter, if you can believe that."

He held up a grocery bag heavy with several pounds of something inside. Square boxes were evident inside the thin plastic bag once he'd finished uncovering himself and moved toward us. Ordinary butter in a normal grocery bag. That's all.

"Hope you're enjoying the food," he said.

"We are, very much," George replied and he stood and shook David's hand and introduced us. "Is Marc with you?"

"Marc had a family problem to take care of."

"Nothing serious, I hope," George said.

"I'm not sure. He asked me to make you comfortable and say he'd meet you at the cottage," he glanced up at one of the high windows. I followed his gaze. "You might want to get going soon. Weather's a mess out there. In fact, I see the president of the bridge club over there sitting with my wife. She should be heading home, too."

"He's right, George," I said, rising from the table and gathering my gear.

"Let me walk you out," David said.

On the way to the exit, we stopped at one of the tables where four women were playing bridge. David laid a hand on one woman's shoulder. "George and Willa Carson, this is my wife, Molly. And her sisters, Maureen Richards and Madeline Trevor, and our good friend Jeannine Montgomery."

Madeline Trevor gave me a strange look I couldn't decipher, but the others were friendly enough. We smiled and nodded all around before David explained the blizzard. "You might want to get folks to wrap it up and head home while they can still get there," he said.

We paid the bill and trudged out to the parking lot along with everyone else.

I started the Jeep and turned on the heat while George used the snowbrush to sweep off the windows. David might not have been the killer, but he drove a snowmobile and was out of the building for a while. I wasn't ready to cross him off my list of suspects just yet. At least I'd talk to Marc about him first.

CHAPTER ELEVEN

AS DAVID HAD WARNED, the blizzard's force had steadily increased while we were at the Cafe and now at least four inches of fresh snow covered the streets. Neither of us had driven on snow in years and no, it's not like riding a bike.

Marc Clayton lived in an historic Victorian mansion on Foxglove Street, not far from Eagle Creek. The mansion's guesthouse would be our home for the week.

George took it slow and easy and eventually, we reached our destination. Marc had said he'd be back later but had left the cottage door unlocked for us. We unpacked and tromped our way inside.

I wandered around the charming cottage, examining everything, which didn't take long. Two minutes to tour the entire place.

A cheerful blaze burned in the fieldstone fireplace and freshly baked cookies scented the air. A single bedroom, small kitchen, one bath and an all-purpose room for everything else. The refrigerator had been stocked with my favorite Cuban coffee and the bar contained Glenfiddich scotch for George and

Bombay Sapphire gin for me. Marc, an excellent host, had once again thought of everything.

George had walked into the bedroom and plopped down on the bed. "Willa, this is supposed to be a vacation. I need a nap." He wiggled his eyebrows at me, but I was most definitely not in the mood.

For the next week, George and I would have more time together than we'd spent in years. When we'd planned the trip, we'd expected a romantic getaway, but romance and murder rarely mix. So much for plans.

I laid down next to George on the bed and snuggled up for warmth, though. In a few minutes, he was snoring.

When I closed my eyes, I could still see Leo Richards' body slumped over the steering wheel of his Toyota, with a gaping hole in his head through which his life had blasted out.

I imagined the young widow and the young fatherless daughter in mourning.

They'd know by now. Someone would have delivered the horrible message that daddy would not be coming home. Their vague images solidified into vivid pictures behind my heavy eyelids. The stuff nightmares are made of.

George slept and eventually I must have dozed off until a solid, continuous pounding on the cottage door pulled me back to the land of the living.

My eyes popped open and I gave my head a quick, negative shake. I moved a little bit closer to George, but the space next to me was empty and the sheets were cold.

Several more knocks suggested that whoever was at the door wasn't about to leave and George wasn't answering the summons for some reason.

I pushed myself out of bed, slipped my feet into shoes,

pulled my sweater tighter around my body and noted George's absence from the tiny abode as I made my way to the front door.

"Where the hell did he go?" I said to the empty room. I took a quick look around, but I didn't see a note.

I pulled back the curtain and peeked out to see the blizzard was now causing a near white-out.

A Michigan State Trooper stood on the porch poised to knock again. I yanked the door open and a strong gust pelted my body with icy snow.

CHAPTER TWELVE

"MA'AM," TROOPER KEMP SAID. He was covered in snow, holding two tall hot cups in black gloved hands. He tipped his head in a gesture of respect and raised one of the cups in my direction. "May I come in? I brought the best coffee in town. I heard you were a caffeine addict."

"Heard from whom?" I asked as I stepped out of the way.

When Kemp was inside and we were snugged up against the elements again, I opened my coffee and he opened the second cup for himself. The double whiff made me swoon. Someone in this town knew how to brew, thank God.

"You must be feeling a little like Typhoid Mary right at the moment," he said after a suitable time for savoring. I looked at him blankly. "You show up here for the first time in ten years and somebody ends up dead."

I said nothing.

His tone was light, teasing. "Does this happen everywhere you go? Or just in Pleasant Harbor?"

My gaze narrowed. So he'd been investigating me. Which is what I should have been doing to him and the victim instead of sleeping. While it was true that I'd had more brushes with murder than most judges, I was in no mood for his humor. I wanted some answers and I wanted them now.

"You've figured out who I am, I take it?"

"Yes ma'am, I have, United States District Judge Wilhelmina Carson. And I also know you have no jurisdiction here." He simply stated the facts. His tone had not turned to belligerence. Yet. But I could feel him going in that direction, which was fine with me. Bring it on.

The jousting restored my equilibrium a bit, although my brain remained fogged with sleep. "All right, then you know that I am not involved in any crimes."

"Never thought you were."

"So tell me what's going on. I think I have a right to know, don't you?"

"Last time we met, I'd have said no, you don't have a right to know. You're a citizen here, like everybody else. You're not even a witness. Nothing but a bystander who found a body. So I'd have said you were entitled to exactly nothing."

Hard to argue with the facts. "I hear a 'but' coming."

"But that was before I talked to Judge Trevor." He flashed a canary-eating grin.

The caffeine hadn't kicked in yet so it took me half a beat longer than it should have to make the connection.

Randy Trevor.

I'd forgotten he was a judge here now. He was a couple of years senior to me at the firm in Detroit where we'd spent our attack-puppy lawyer years. We'd worked on cases together at the bottom of the totem pole before he and his wife, Madeline, decided to move north to Pleasant Harbor to be near both families. He figured he'd get a faster boost up the career ladder here in his home town and he'd been right. He was appointed to the bench long before I was. From time to time we'd chatted at legal events, but otherwise we hadn't spoken to each other in years.

And it must have been Madeline Trevor who was at the bridge club this afternoon. The woman who'd given me the strange look. The president who so intimidated the hostess. Probably her sisters at the table with her, too.

Kemp nodded when he sensed I'd figured things out. Then he continued, "Judge Trevor wants to see you. He asked me to escort you to his chambers."

While it was true that I had no jurisdiction here, Randy Trevor couldn't compel me to show up in his fiefdom, either. This was a request. Nothing more. Whether he phrased it like one or not. "Did he say why?"

"No ma'am, he didn't. But I suspect he's looking for some experienced help here. We don't have murders like this in Pleasant Harbor. This isn't Detroit. Or even Tampa." Kemp sipped his coffee while he waited for me to agree.

"You've got resources at your disposal, surely."

"We do."

"Why not ask for assistance from one of your colleagues, then?"

Kemp shrugged.

Which was okay. I figured I knew the answer to this one. The situation was similar to a man asking for directions. A very powerful man. A man used to making decisions and telling people what to do. In other words, hell would absolutely freeze over before he'd admit to his colleagues that he needed anything, let alone ask for help on a case if he could get some secret talent off the books.

Which meant I held all the control here. Or at least, control over the next couple of hours.

The way I saw it, I could refuse, which was totally against my nature and wasn't really an option. I'm not one to stand on the sidelines much. Randy Trevor would have remembered that about me. Option two: I could go into a meeting completely ignorant of the situation to joust with a man I didn't really know any more and who did have jurisdiction and probably access to more information than I could get quickly on my own. Better choice: I could wheedle a bit more information from Trooper Kemp before I made up my mind.

The warm coffee I held in my hands seemed to beckon me. I sat at the kitchen table and gestured Kemp toward the other chair as I sipped, stalling, running through things in my head.

I hadn't recovered from the bloody visions behind my closed eyelids during my nap. George had probably walked over to the mansion and he'd be back shortly. He'd be willing to drive in the blizzard, maybe. I loved to drive on the open road with the convertible top down on my car in Tampa. But driving in blizzards and whiteouts? No thanks.

"You know what's going on here, don't you?" I asked. Kemp didn't confirm, but he didn't deny, either. He just drank his coffee and waited. "Don't you think I deserve to be on an equal playing field with everyone else?"

He took his gloves off and got comfortable in the chair, but he kept the big brimmed hat on. I watched him think about things.

After a bit, he said, "Leo Richards, the fellow you found this morning? The murder victim?"

I nodded.

"The situation is a bit more curious than you know. Because

he's been missing for more than a year. Almost fourteen months, to be precise."

"What do you mean?"

"He'd been having financial trouble on top of some other family problems and you know how that puts stress on a marriage. January was a year ago, he and his wife had a major blowout. Broken furniture, holes punched in the wall, the whole nine yards. Her sisters were there and all three of them were terrified. He left the house in anger, jumped into that Toyota SUV you almost slammed, and—" he shrugged again.

"He didn't even try to contact his child in all that time?"

"Wife says not."

"What about his job?"

"He had a partner in his hardware business who hasn't seen him in the past fourteen months, either. David Mason. I believe you met him earlier today at Eagle Creek Cafe, didn't you?" Kemp continued to drink his coffee but he watched me closely. How did he know where we ate lunch or that we met Mason?

Somehow, his research on me had included where we went after we left him at the murder scene. That was the important piece of Intel.

"Where did Richards go when he left town?"

"We don't know. Las Vegas, Atlantic City, Detroit. Wherever he could find a casino or a poker table, would be my guess," Kemp said.

"He was addicted to gambling?"

Kemp nodded. "Caused him and his family no end of grief, I can tell you."

Probably created quite a few local enemies, too. Some of them might even be capable of murder. "Did you try to locate him after he disappeared?"

"He's a grown man. If he wants to desert his family, there's no law against it as far as I know. Not the sort of thing we'd conduct a nation-wide manhunt over, anyway."

"Makes him a deadbeat dad and a sorry human being, though," I said.

"You got that right."

"Didn't the wife try to find him?"

"The family hired a couple of private investigators, I'm told. But they didn't find the guy. People don't want to be found, there are still lots of ways to hide in this country."

"If that's what happened," I said. People are kidnapped for ransom or human trafficking or any number of reasons. But Leo Richards might not fit those victim profiles. I'd need to know a lot more about him than I did now to figure that out.

"Meaning what?"

"There should have been a plane ticket or something," I replied.

"Maybe," he shrugged again. He waited a beat, "Like I told you before, this is a small town. He didn't come home and never went back to work and nobody has seen him since then. He'd ruined a lot of lives already. I'm not sure people cared much about him by then. Guy's gone and good riddance, you know?"

I took a sip of coffee and almost spit it back. Stone cold. I hated reheated coffee, but I needed warm liquid and now was not the time to get all precious about my caffeine. I popped the cup into the microwave for a couple of minutes.

While I waited, I shook my head to clear it of sleep's last cobwebs and asked, "Did you check the mileage? On the Toyota?"

"Yes."

"Loquacious, aren't you?"

"I try."

I grinned. I didn't want to like the guy, but it was hard not to. "And? What did you find out?"

Kemp said, "Well, that's a curious thing, too. The Toyota is about ten years old. Like most vehicles around here, it's got a lot of miles on it. Close to two-hundred thousand. His wife says Leo had the vehicle serviced a few days or so before he disappeared. We checked with the mechanic. He said Leo always took good care of the Toyota and the mileage was close to two-hundred thousand last time he serviced it."

The microwave dinged. I pulled out the cup and took a sip of the heated coffee and burned my tongue. "Crap!" I drew a cold glass of water and swished it around in my mouth, which seemed to help my scalded tongue not one whit.

Kemp looked at his watch. "Judge Trevor is expecting us. We can talk about the rest in the car. Are you going dressed like that?"

Which is when I looked down and noticed I was wearing my pajamas under my cardigan. Now how the hell had that happened? George. Obviously. I hoped.

"I'll be right back," I said, as I ducked into the bedroom to slip into my jeans again. It took me only a few seconds to dress in the warmest clothes I owned. I ran a quick toothbrush around my teeth and finger-combed my pixie-cut. I looked again for a note from George, but found none. In three minutes, I was ready. George says I'm fast, for a girl.

I snagged my parka, gloves, and my miniscule purse and dropped my phone into my pocket, wishing I'd remembered to stick it on the charger before my nap. When I returned to the front door to don the hideously huge boots, Kemp was waiting.

"Do you have any theories about who shot Richards?" I

asked him with my hand on the knob and before we opened the door to the blasting snow once more.

"Prevailing theory is the guy the media has been calling the snow sniper."

I halted at the threshold with the door open and the howling wind rushing through, snow swirling around my body. "The what?"

"Let's go. I'll tell you about him in the car." Kemp gave me a little push on the shoulder which made me plant my feet inside the cottage.

"I'm driving my own car," I said.

He laughed and pressed my shoulder forward again knocking me slightly over the threshold where I planted my feet more firmly. He pulled on his gloves. "That'll be some trick. Even if you could navigate in this blizzard. Which I doubt."

I didn't budge. "I've got four-wheel drive and I've driven in blizzards before, Kemp."

He sobered quickly at my steely tone and fierce stare and unrelenting stubbornness. "Yes, ma'am. I'm sure you do and you have. But not today. Because your vehicle's already gone."

I whipped my head around to peer through the white stuff. Sure enough, the driven snow covered everything. Trees, shrubs, trash cans. Everything that is except the missing Jeep.

George Carson. Where the hell did you go?

Kemp gave me a little shoulder nudge again and this time, I stepped out into the storm. He followed me and pulled the cottage door closed. Then he moved around in front of me and led the way to his cruiser, which was now as snow-covered as everything else.

Kemp opened the passenger door and I slipped inside. He closed me snuggly within the cold cruiser and trudged around the front and slipped in behind the wheel. Now that he'd secured me inside the car, he honored his promise to tell me more without prompting. "I'm not sure how Leo Richards was involved with the snow sniper. Maybe there was no relationship between the two at all. As far as we can tell, the sniper killed the other three victims randomly. One thing I just found out a few minutes ago, though."

He fired up the ignition and waited for a bit of warmth before he flipped on the wipers. They struggled to move the heavy snow aside. Maybe he didn't have a snowbrush. "We got the quick and dirty preliminary ballistics report back on the bullet used to kill Leo Richards."

Those quick reports could be wrong. But they could rule out possibilities and narrow the search for the murder weapon. I reached to fasten my seat belt. I was colder than I'd been in years and when I managed to get warm again, I vowed to stay as far away from snow as humanly possible for the rest of my life. Of course, I'd vowed that before and here I was. "What did the ballistics establish?"

"The gun that killed Leo Richards was not the gun used on any of the snow sniper's other victims," he said, reaching his arm out the window and catching the wiper to knock the snow off.

"Did you tell Judge Trevor about that report?"

"Yes, ma'am. Just before I knocked on your door. Doesn't mean the guy owns only one gun, though, you know?" he replied, half a second before he flipped the fan up to full blast on the defroster. After that, all conversation was lost in the wind.

CHAPTER THIRTEEN

BY THE TIME WE headed out of the cottage driveway, we could almost see through the tiny clear space on the bottom of the windshield.

Kemp concentrated on his driving and I thought about what to ask first when we could turn the blasting fan down low enough to hear each other. I wanted to know about the snow sniper and why he was a suspect when the ballistics were wrong on the murder weapon and whether Kemp had any leads and when the sniper would be arrested and a zillion other questions.

But I didn't want him to lose concentration while driving on the snow and black ice my experience said was probably underneath it. So I held my tongue and looked at the slowly passing landscape while I made my mental interrogation list.

The world outside the vehicle resembled a snow globe, everything shaken upside down and filled with the blizzard. The town was picturesque and remote and the pristine white snow covered everything ugly underneath.

What rot lay under the beautiful blanket of false serenity falling softly all around me, making travel difficult and clarity impossible? This was a place where a man could disappear for an entire year and no one mourned or seemed to care. Pleasant Harbor was not so idyllic after all.

Snow continued to fall steadily and Kemp had trouble keeping us between the ditches even in the four-wheel drive vehicle and even without my distracting questions. So my inquisition was delayed.

I pulled out my cell phone, which hadn't rung since we arrived here. Not even once. Today was Tuesday and my courtroom should have been in full swing in the Florida sunshine. My assistant, Augustus, had promised not to call me with trivial questions, but I hadn't believed him. He'd never honored that promise before. There was no reason to think he'd start doing so now.

I pulled off one of the clumsy gloves to glance at the phone's screen. One missed call. Okay. At least I wasn't completely out of touch. The call was from George's cell. He'd left a voicemail. I pushed the button and held the phone to my ear.

The signal had been weak and the message was garbled and cut off too soon. I listened to it three times before I was able to make out a few words that sounded maybe like "…Sorry I didn't leave a note…. Couldn't sleep…. Back soon."

Otherwise, nothing.

I pushed the redial and got a lot of empty air. I tried the internet browser to look up media coverage of the snow sniper, but couldn't connect to that, either. No signals. Which wasn't surprising I guess, given the abominable weather.

I dropped the phone back into my pocket and returned my

gaze to peering outside at the blinding white trail ahead of Kemp's squad car.

"What the hell is going on here?" I didn't realize I'd asked aloud until he replied.

"Classic misdirection, I'd say. Wouldn't you?" He held the wheel in a tight grip at the nine and three positions. His body leaned forward as if getting closer to the windshield would improve visibility outside. The cruiser's headlights seemed to make matters worse because they simply illuminated the heavy snow, but Kemp might have thought they made the cruiser more obvious to others and we needed them to avoid a collision or something.

Before I had a chance to ask another question, he raised his voice to say, "The snow sniper is a rather fanciful moniker, but the media types do like to give these killers a handle. The short of it is that we've had three murders in Mid-Michigan before this one, all three had similar characteristics and all were committed by the same weapon. This one is either a change in the killer's method and weapon or it's a copycat."

"Copycat seems the most logical since the ballistics don't match, doesn't it?" I was almost shouting to be heard over the blasting fan and the struggling windshield wipers.

"Probably. There are other differences, too."

"Such as?"

"One thing is the snow sniper has targeted victims from a longer range using a rifle. This one seemed like a rifle shot, but it wasn't. This murder was very up close and personal. And this is the first victim we've found dead in a vehicle. The others were exposed to the shot. One snowmobiler, a cross-country skier, and a woman at a car wash. Fewer logistical issues when the victim isn't surrounded by a steel enclosure."

"I take it these details were withheld from the media? Otherwise, how would a copycat think he could make so many changes and get away with them?"

"I'm a cop, not a mind reader." Kemp might have shrugged, but inside the heavy jacket it was hard to tell. "The good news is that we identified the snow sniper a couple of days ago, but we were still collecting evidence and hadn't arrested him yet. If he killed Richards, then the bad news is another man is dead and we're all looking damn stupid right now. The somewhat better news is that the Richards murder gave us the probable cause we needed to get tight warrants. There's a team on the way to pick him up in Grand Rapids now. So we should know soon enough whether he also owns the Leo Richards murder weapon."

"But you think the snow sniper didn't kill Richards. Aside from wishful thinking, got any evidence?"

Kemp said nothing. Neither did I. He'd answer my question or I wouldn't say another word.

The silence lasted until we finally reached the Pleasant County Courthouse. We'd traveled the three-mile distance in about half an hour, according to the digital clock in the dash. Not bad, considering the road conditions.

When Kemp pulled into the parking lot, I was relieved to see a county snow plow. Kemp slid into a plowed parking space and turned off the ignition, creating an abrupt and unnerving quiet inside the cabin.

Silently, I pried my hands apart, flexed my shoulders and stretched my neck from side to side, trying to return some blood flow to my severely cramped muscles.

After a moment, Kemp said, "Ready to go?"

I said nothing and didn't move.

He tried to nudge me along. "We're already late. Judge

Trevor will explain everything to you when we get inside."

"Tell me why you don't think the snow sniper killed Leo Richards or I'm not going in there. You know the answer. He knows, too. And I don't. We level that playing field right now."

"Actually, you know everything Judge Trevor knows. You're already on that level playing field. Let's go."

I didn't move.

Kemp pulled off his glove and wiped his face with his hand while he thought things through. His research on me must have given him a few examples of exactly how stubborn I can be because as the silence lingered, he took me at my word.

"The murder weapon was a Desert Eagle 50 caliber handgun. Reported stolen last year. It's a match. No doubt about it. That's the weapon that killed Leo Richards this morning."

There was more. I could feel it. "A match to what? And what's the rest of the story?"

He didn't say. I didn't budge.

Kemp sighed. Weary, maybe. Resigned at least. "The weapon was registered to David Mason."

"That's your big secret? David Mason, the chef at Eagle Creek Cafe? His stolen gun was the murder weapon?"

"That's the one. Now let's go." Before I could ask any more questions, Kemp left the cruiser, closing me alone inside. I saw him pulling his gloves over his hands.

After snugging up my gloves, I opened the door and stepped into the blizzard again. Why the hell had I ever thought this frozen white stuff was the least bit romantic?

My boots landed onto a layer of new snow over the hard pack. The wind nearly knocked me over. My hair became covered with snowflakes in just a brief moment and the icy flakes pelted my face. I flipped up the parka's hood and turned my head down in self-defense.

Kemp walked around the back of the vehicle. I could hear his boots crunching on the snow beside me, but I'd have had to turn my entire body to see him with the parka's hood up. He didn't lock the cruiser, probably because he was afraid the locks would freeze. Or maybe he figured if any fool was willing to come out in this storm to steal the damn thing, they could have it.

"The entrance is this way, Judge." He steadied me by a tight grip on my arm and we made our way cautiously around the building. Kemp pulled hard on the handle of the glass door, sweeping a foot of snow off the entranceway as the door's rubber flashing scraped the concrete and it pivoted open.

I rushed inside and he followed.

After we stamped and dusted off, without another word Kemp led the way down a corridor to our left. We passed two large dark wood doors over which the words "Courtroom A" were posted in brass letters.

The next doorway had white opaque glass on the top half and wood on the bottom half. The kind of doors you see in old movies from the 1940s. Black letters stood out boldly on the white opaque glass. *Judge Randy Trevor, Pleasant County Circuit Judge.*

Kemp rang a small doorbell to the right. A female voice spoke through the intercom above the button.

"Yes?"

"Trooper Justin Kemp to see Judge Trevor."

A buzzer sounded and Kemp ushered me through another door.

CHAPTER FOURTEEN

WE ENTERED INTO A roomy reception area. The woman who had answered the buzzer sat behind an antique wood desk. Although the building and the office furnishings were old-fashioned, her desk held a thoroughly modern telephone system and better computer equipment than I'd had in Tampa's old federal courthouse before I was allowed to move into newer quarters.

Judge Trevor's secretary, though, could have come from central casting for the same 1940s movie that furnished the office. She looked as if she had been sitting at this very desk since the building was constructed. She was probably sixty years old, but she looked ninety.

She had blue-gray hair, worn in a style that required a once weekly visit to the salon for a shampoo and set. Glasses so old-fashioned they were trendy framed her eyes, giving her the look of a startled cat. Her white cardigan was held around her shoulders by a sweater clip of plastic pearls. She wore a floral perfume that was vaguely familiar but I couldn't name because my sense of smell was now frozen.

The entire effect was surreal, as if I'd stepped back in time when I crossed that last threshold. I almost expected an old film star to come out of the door to the Judge's chambers any second.

"Hello, Sue," Kemp said in a sweeter tone than I'd heard him utilize until now. "This is Judge Wilhelmina Carson, from Florida. She's staying over at Marc Clayton's guest cottage. We need to see Judge Trevor." Why it was necessary to share all of this information with Sue was beyond me, but I was the guest here.

Sue Evans didn't greet me cheerfully or kindly or in any other way. I might have been invisible for all of the attention she paid to me.

"He's on the phone. Have a seat," she said, barely taking her gaze from the computer screen. I stood near enough to her desk to see she was reading newspaper accounts of the snow sniper's kills. I read over her shoulder, glad that she had enlarged the print about two-hundred percent.

The headline was "Snow Sniper Kills Third Victim at Bayside Carwash." The photographs were winter scenes. Both were exterior views of a do-it-yourself wash stall. A silver mini-van was parked just outside the stall, doors and hatch open, near the coin-operated vacuum cleaner. The vacuum hose rested inside the mini-van's open back hatch. Something dark had stained the carpet, probably blood.

The victim's picture was a grainy formal portrait probably made by an old camera using film. I couldn't read the screen as well as I needed to, but I made out that the victim was shot by a rifle and died instantly. Her identity was withheld pending notification to the family.

One shell casing had been located, but police weren't sure whether the casing was relevant at the time.

Two other shootings were rapidly summarized at the end. One victim was a man sitting on a snowmobile in a parking lot of a convenience store. The other was a woman who had been cross-country skiing. Her body hadn't been discovered for several hours because of her remote location.

Sue must have felt me leaning behind her because she turned and glared at me before she picked up the phone receiver and said, "Trooper Kemp and Judge Carson are here to see you."

A booming, disembodied male voice I recognized even after all these years responded, "Send them in."

Sue inclined her head toward a wooden door on the other side of a latched wood gate. A long buzzer sounded as Trooper Kemp took my elbow again and guided me through. I was beginning to feel like I'd fallen into another world, somehow. A place too quiet, too old, with too many secrets.

When we entered his chambers, Judge Randy Trevor was moving from behind his desk, making his way toward us.

"Willa! It's so good to see you!" Instead of offering to shake hands, he leaned in for a big hug and a tight squeeze that I could barely feel through the parka. He greeted me as if I was a long-lost best friend, when we had only been co-workers a long time ago. I'd never received a warmer greeting from a colleague, including him, even back when we actually knew each other. All of which made me feel suspicious instead of welcomed. What was going on here?

The amenities dispensed with, seated behind his desk with Kemp and me across from him, Judge Trevor got right to the point. "Thanks for coming, Willa. When I saw Justin this afternoon, and he told me you were here, I asked him to see you."

"So he said," I replied.

Kemp had removed his big brimmed hat. Close-cropped red hair and pink scalp, a small nose, freckles across the bridge, a good smile and a pleasant demeanor emerged from the brim's shadow. He seemed wholesome. Under better circumstances, I thought I'd like Justin Kemp quite a lot.

Randy Trevor sat with both elbows on the arms of his chair, his hands clasped together, looking down as if he were praying. Maybe he was. If my jurisdiction was beset by such a killer, I would've been.

"What do you make of all of this Willa?" he asked. "You were always good at figuring things out. Justin tells me you discovered the body this morning. What did you see that we might have missed? What's going on here in my sleepy little town?"

Everyone in Pleasant Harbor knew everyone else. Odds were that the killer was not a stranger to anyone, either. Which meant that Trevor could be involved in all of this somehow. Kemp and Sue Evans, too. My experience and my gut said so, even if the evidence didn't. Yet.

Trevor's professional involvement was fine, albeit premature. No one had been arrested yet and until a suspect was in custody, his role was not official.

Maybe he was curious. Dedicated, perhaps. After all, I had no official role here, either. And yet here I sat. Because Trevor made it so. No one in Tampa would have had that kind of power over me or anyone on our police force. Yet Trevor and others believed he had that power here. Good to know.

I shrugged. "I'm a visitor, Randy. All I know is that you have some pretty bizarre stuff going on in this 'sleepy little town.'" I mimicked his inflection on the last three words. He probably thought I was being snide. I probably was.

Trevor considered something for a few seconds and seemed to make a decision of his own. "Would you mind waiting for us outside, Justin?" Kemp nodded, doing Trevor's bidding once again. How far could Kemp be trusted? I heard the door close behind me.

Judge Trevor leaned forward, placing both forearms on his desk, and refolded his hands into the prayer position. He looked at me with the earnest expression I could remember so clearly it felt like a flashback to an earlier time. A time before snow snipers and murder victims and blizzards and my missing husband. A time when I had nothing to fear from Randy Trevor and he had nothing to fear from me. A lifetime ago.

"Pleasant Harbor *was* a sleepy little town when I moved here ten years ago," he said, ignoring my snide remark. "We've grown a lot since then. Our population, year-round, is low five digits but that's misleading. We get tourists now, winter and summer, sufficient to swell the number of folks to at least ten thousand every weekend."

He raised his water glass and took a sip, then settled more comfortably in his chair. I thought he might actually put his feet on the desk like he regularly did when we were associates, but he didn't.

"What's your point?" I said.

He glared a bit. I was getting under his skin. Good. He might make a mistake I could exploit if he wasn't too comfortable. "Now we have all the problems any other big city has. I get the *New York Times* delivered to my house every day. My wife wears couture clothes and carries expensive handbags when we go to dinner. And we've got so much crime these days that we're building a big new jail and courthouse complex to deal with it all."

I shrugged. Whatever he thought would impress me in that speech had missed the mark. "My jurisdiction covers several big cities, Randy. But even in Tampa we don't let snipers get away with murder and go on their merry way until the next unlucky motorist happens past."

This time my tone had been more than snide. I was insulting and I didn't really care. He'd hijacked me, not the other way around. He owed me answers, at the very least. I owed him nothing.

Trevor jerked his head back sharply. He was a big man about town here, probably not used to disrespect of any kind. But to me he was just another guy with a government job. Meaning he worked for us, not the other way around. And he was not half as important as he seemed to think. Not to me, anyway.

I rose from my chair. "I've got things to do."

He waived me back. "Okay. Okay."

I gave him my best get-to-the-point stare. The one that works on recalcitrant defendants in my courtroom a lot better than his methods were working on me.

I sat on the edge of the seat this time, letting him see I wasn't making myself too comfortable, the better to get up and go if he didn't stop jerking me around.

CHAPTER FIFTEEN

HE SWIPED HIS HAIR with his open left-hand and a weary sigh escaped his mouth. "It's been hard for David Mason these last few years. He was just getting on his feet again."

So Kemp had lied to me. Trevor did know about the ballistics report after all. He knew David Mason's stolen gun was used to murder Leo Richards. He thought David had done the deed.

"David's family was just coming out of a really bad patch after his business partner gambled away all their assets and disappeared."

Yeah, yeah, yeah. I was a little too tired of the excuses. "And then what?" I prodded.

Trevor sighed again. He stood and began to pace the room, slowly, as if he was creating his story as he went. "I'm not sure exactly. I know that people didn't trust him. He'd had trouble paying his employees. David went to work over at the cafe, which pays enough to keep the wolf from the door, I guess."

"What does any of this have to do with Leo Richards' murder? Or with me, for that matter?"

Trevor bowed his head again briefly before he looked up to give me a steady gaze. "Leo Richards was David's business partner. He's the one who destroyed David and his family. And then he just vanished months ago and left David to handle the mess."

"And David couldn't handle it," I said. "So you're saying David Mason had a good reason to kill Richards, then. Your case is solved. You should be telling Kemp this story instead of me."

Trevor stopped and stared at me with a stunned expression I took to be surprise. "You don't know?" Then, he caught himself and resumed a weary tone. "Not that it matters. Everyone knows."

I waited. He'd spit it out or he wouldn't. I didn't care one way or the other and I didn't see why he'd think I might care.

"David Mason is my brother-in-law. His wife and my wife are sisters," Trevor said.

The weary countenance didn't impress me. I was weary, too. George was missing and I couldn't make it back to the cottage alone. I felt trapped physically, emotionally and intellectually and I struggled against the restraints.

"When did you find out David was coming unraveled?"

Trevor removed his hand from his pocket and wiped his face. "Three weeks ago. David became more and more frantic. Three weeks wouldn't have been a problem, if this was the first time he'd been unable to pay his bills. People are neighborly here. Creditors would have let him slide."

But of course, it wasn't the first time. Far from it, I'd bet.

"People who had been burned before were unwilling to give him a chance. What could he do?" He actually looked at me with innocence in his eyes, as if his excuses for his brother-in-law's criminal behavior were remotely acceptable.

Now it was my turn to be incredulous. And pissed off. "Besides kill Leo Richards you mean?" I stood up and turned to stalk out.

In a flash he was behind me. He grabbed my arm. "Wait," he pleaded. "Please."

I looked at him. "For what?" He still held my arm. I looked down pointedly at the hand he'd placed to restrain me.

He did not let go. "There is a snow sniper, Willa. The State Police will arrest him today. He killed three people already. He could have killed Leo Richards, too. The snow sniper is a more likely suspect than David. He's killed three times before. *Three times.* He'll be convicted. It won't take long. He could have killed a fourth time. Maybe he did. I need your help, Willa. Will you help me?"

No, I wanted to scream, *I will not help you. And if you don't do your job, I'll make sure you pay for Richards' murder, too. Remember Richard Nixon. It's not the crime, it's the cover up.*

But I didn't say that.

And because I said nothing, he continued, "David Mason is not a bad man, Willa, but he is a desperate one. I know you see desperate people in your courtroom all the time, because I do. Desperate people do desperate things." Still he held my arm, restraining my freedom, making me angrier by the millisecond. "David has a wife. Small children. His family needs him."

As if that made David's actions somehow less heinous, less destructive.

"Leo Richards had a wife and a daughter, too. You took an oath to uphold the law just like I did, Randy," I told him, shaking my arm so that he'd let me go. "Are you going to do that? Or do I have to do it for you?"

If George and I hadn't stumbled upon the crime scene, David

might have escaped detection completely. By the time Kemp arrived at the Toyota this morning, most of the exterior forensic evidence had already been destroyed. Perhaps it would all have been gone, even the ballistics. Randy Trevor would have had his way.

The mere idea heated up my anger like one of those steam tunnels under the old asylum. I was near ready to blow.

What Randy and David had planned seemed like the perfect crime. Randy knew the snow sniper had been identified and would be arrested with just a little bit more evidence. He might have told David about it or maybe David just got lucky with the timing. Either way, David killed Leo thinking the snow sniper would be blamed. His insurance against prison was his brother in law, the one and only judge.

In a town like Pleasant Harbor, Judge Randy Trevor would have enough clout to make something like this go away for David, if David was arrested at all. Trevor shouldn't preside over a case involving his brother-in-law, but who would object? If no one challenged him, there were any number of ways he could have helped David avoid conviction. But if all those methods failed, Trevor could simply give David Mason a suspended sentence, too.

Was my old colleague that corrupt? Would he do that? I could see in his eyes that he would.

"Forget it, Randy. I was there. I saw Leo Richards' brains blown all to hell. David brought the gun and set up the crime. Maybe he didn't mean to kill Leo, but he intended to threaten him, at the very least." I gathered my coat and pulled my gloves out of the deep pocket. "If you think I'm going to let David get away with murder, you have another think coming," I told him as I turned, once again, toward the door.

Trevor put both hands into his pockets and walked around me. He opened the door so that I could walk out. Loud enough for Sue and Kemp to hear, he said "Thank you for coming, Judge Carson." In slightly sinister tones, or at least that's how it sounded to me, he said, "I won't forget this."

I raised my voice slightly to be sure everyone within earshot could hear. "Neither will I. I've been home-towned by better men than you, Randy. Check it out if you doubt my word. Don't get in my way."

We glared at each other half a moment more before I stalked out.

Kemp followed close behind me as I strode through Judge Trevor's outer office and began the trek across the parking lot. Outside, snow continued to fall in heavy, wet flakes. At least another inch of the white barricade had accumulated since he'd parked the cruiser. Could I walk three miles back to the cottage without freezing to death? Maybe not. But I would damn sure try.

I kicked at the snow and watched it pile up on my boots. The snow was my enemy now, keeping me captive here in this silently hostile world, away from George, away from my beloved Florida sunshine.

Neither Kemp nor I said anything more until we reached the cruiser. As I marched past the door, he laid a restraining hand on my shoulder and I shook it off.

"Don't be so stubborn for once. You'll freeze out here and you won't find a ride in this weather. I can take you back to your cottage, but you know you'll be stuck there until this weather clears. You can't drive anywhere." I kept moving, even as I knew he was right. He grabbed my arm and spun me around to face him. "You'll never get there. Let me drive you. I brought you here. I feel responsible for you."

I said nothing. Was Kemp under Judge Trevor's control now? I'd be a fool to assume otherwise.

"I've lived here all my life, Willa. I know these roads. The county tries, but the plows can't keep up with this much snowfall." He released my arm and opened the passenger door.

CHAPTER SIXTEEN

I WANTED TO KEEP walking, to ignore him, to make it back under my own steam. But I knew he was right. I was more likely to die trying. So I said nothing and struggled into the front seat. He closed me inside and walked around the back of the cruiser.

He settled into the driver's seat, put the key into the ignition and turned it. The cruiser roared to life. He flipped on the windshield wipers, throwing heavy snow onto the ground. Next, he turned up the fan, full blast, and we watched as the cold air fogged the windshield from the inside.

It was the last straw.

The events of the day finally broke through my forced composure.

"Shit!" I said, slamming my hand down on the dash. "How can anybody live in this godforsaken place?"

To my astonishment, Kemp threw back his head and roared with laughter. I stared at him as if he had declared himself a lunatic.

"What's so damn funny?"

He collected himself, but his eyes teared with the effort of contained laughter. "I'm sorry. It's just that—"

"What?" I snapped at him. I grabbed for the door handle to stalk out, or as close to stalking as possible in thigh deep snow, but he didn't move.

"Well, look around you," he gestured a wide arc with his arm. "It's beautiful here. The snow makes everything look like a storybook village."

"Not to me, it doesn't," I told him in a stern tone that sobered his humor quickly. "I see a place where people get killed in their cars. And their killers get away with it."

I bit back my words and didn't say *and threatened by judges* because I wasn't ready to share that with Kemp or anyone else just yet. I needed to sort out how to handle that for myself first. I'd warned Randy Trevor off. But he was dangerous and I didn't know how far he would go. I wasn't afraid of him, but I wasn't ready to take him on, even though I'd told him otherwise.

I tried again to open the door, but Kemp had pushed the door locks and held me captive.

"Look," Kemp said, glancing down at his watch. "It's dark out, already after five o'clock. My shift is over. What if we grab a quick dinner and then I'll make sure you get back and settled in for the night."

I wanted to find George and drive down to Traverse City and catch the first flight out of here. I wanted to sit next to George and hold his hand and talk to him. I wanted to be there when his eyes twinkled and he said, "Hey, what's up, Mighty Mouse?"

But I didn't know where George was or when he would be back. Kemp was right. Again. Dammit. Why had I never listened to George when he wanted me to carry a concealed weapon? Stubbornness actually can go too far. Who knew?

Now that the windows were partially clear, I could see the main road in front of the courthouse was snow blocked again. The plows hadn't been by here in at least an hour, and more fresh snow had piled on top of the old, and it was still coming down fast. It would be the same everywhere, only most roads would be even worse.

The wind was starting to whip up, too. Wind would take some of the humidity out of the air and blow drifts across the roads. Treacherous black ice was impossible to see or tame. If I got stuck out there, I could very well freeze to death. I'd be of no use to anyone suffering from frostbite, or worse.

Reluctantly, I had to agree with Kemp.

But I didn't have to like it.

"Come on," Kemp cajoled. "You need to eat. We're not far from Eagle Creek Cafe. You won't find better food anywhere."

He was right on all points. I might as well have a good meal. I hadn't eaten much today and we had scant provisions at the cottage. I'd be at least a little safer in a place where there were other people. And maybe my phone would work in a more populated place and I could get connected and back in control of my life.

"Okay, Kemp. You've worn me down."

He grinned. "And you can call me Justin, Willa. It'll make dinner conversation less ridiculous," he said as he put the cruiser in gear and slowly made our way through the white drifts covering the roads.

Our progress toward Eagle Creek was glacial. He'd popped the cruiser into four-wheel drive, which helped some with traction, but required an even slower pace. We spent half an hour driving and sliding the two miles to the restaurant.

"His wife, Madeline, is the real power behind the throne.

She's got a temper, too. Trevor is an all-around good guy, Willa. He takes care of his family is all. Can't blame a guy for that," Kemp said, eyes staring straight ahead, white knuckled grip on the steering wheel.

"So I figured out," I replied, sarcasm loaded in my tone. I was still mad. Not ready to let my grievances go.

"The family's had a run of bad luck for the past few years," he said.

"*Bad luck?* Is that what you call it around here? Where I'm from, we call that murder and it gets you the death penalty." My hand had a tight grip on the armrest and my feet pressed into the floor helping to keep my balance as Kemp's cruiser struggled and slid and slewed along the snow covered streets.

Kemp glanced briefly toward me, looking for agreement or friendship or something I wasn't prepared to offer. "We don't know that David killed Leo yet. And even if we find out that David did pull the trigger, can you imagine how hard that's got to be on Trevor?"

"Not as hard as it was on Leo Richards, I'll bet," I replied.

"There's six kids involved, you know."

"Six? I'm confused. I thought Leo had two and David had two."

"That's right, but Trevor has two kids also."

"What do the judge's kids have to do with anything? He's sentenced murderers before, surely. His kids have got to know that's his job, even if their friends are involved. Why would they be worried about that?"

"So you'd have Randy Trevor, what, send his brother-in-law to prison and then raise those kids in addition to Leo's and his own?"

"What are you talking about?"

Kemp snorted a little and the corners of his mouth lifted as he nodded his head. "So he didn't tell you, then."

"Didn't tell me what?"

"Trevor didn't tell you that he's related to both David Mason and Leo Richards?"

"He did not. He said Mason and Richards were business partners. He said Mason was his brother-in-law."

"That's all true, as far as it goes. They were business partners, and David is his brother-in-law. But that's not the half of it. Randy Trevor, David Mason and Leo Richards are married to three sisters. This is a tragedy for the entire family, not just a part of the family. They've already lost one husband and father in Leo Richards. You want to send another husband and father to prison in David Mason. And then what? Judge Trevor takes on the whole family?"

So that was Randy Trevor's dilemma. He wanted to protect his wife's family. Judges aren't gods. We have lives. We have families. We have feelings. So his desire was understandable.

But he was a judge. He had responsibilities that came with the job. If he couldn't, or wouldn't fulfill his oath to administer blind justice in this case, the very least he should do was to recuse himself and let an impartial judge take over.

He was using his power for his own self-interest. Which meant he was corrupt. He'd lose his job and be disbarred. Three families would be ruined for sure if Randy Trevor continued down this path.

I said, "The wives aren't helpless, you know. Those six kids have mothers, too."

"You met them all today. At the bridge club. In birth order, Madeline, Maureen, and Molly. The 3Ms, folks call them around here. From an old line Pleasant Harbor family. Did they look like they were capable of taking care of themselves to you?" he replied.

The comment irked me so my words were a bit too testy. "Here's some advice that may save your life, Kemp. Never underestimate a woman. Every cop should know that much."

Kemp grinned and nodded. He'd have tipped his hat again, if he'd been wearing one. "Noted."

I said, "So Leo is married to Maureen, the middle sister from a prominent family. And he's missing for fourteen months. And nobody does anything about that? That doesn't seem reasonable to me. Does it to you?"

Kemp might have shrugged again. He said, "The mileage on the Toyota bothers me more. Even if he only drove down to Traverse City and stashed the vehicle somewhere and flew out and drove back to where we found him, the SUV should have more miles on it."

I thought again about the victim's unusually pink skin. There were only two causes I could think of, and neither one of them made any sense. Too many anomalies in this case, for sure.

We'd finally arrived at Eagle Creek. Kemp's vehicle plowed two fresh ruts through the snow in the parking lot and slammed into a snow pile higher than the cruiser.

CHAPTER SEVENTEEN

MOST PEOPLE HAD ENOUGH sense to stay home on a night like this. But there were two vehicles I recognized parked close to the entrance. A silver Cadillac I'd noticed there earlier today. The other was our rented Jeep. Parked in the same place George had placed it at lunch.

So this is where you are. The knowledge made me feel both better and worse. I was relieved he wasn't dying in a ditch somewhere, of course. But also damned annoyed that he hadn't let me know he was okay. Now that I knew he wasn't dead, I considered killing him myself for scaring me. Figuratively, of course.

I checked my cell phone for messages again. Nothing. The storm must have done something more permanent to the cell network than I'd hoped. I hadn't received a call in the past several hours and I knew both George and Augustus would have tried to reach me.

I dialed George's cell phone, but nothing happened. "Great," I said under my breath to no one. "Just great."

Kemp backed up slightly away from the snow mound, shut

down the wipers and the lights, and turned off the ignition. "Just think about it, Willa. You're a fair judge, they tell me. Find out all the facts before you decide what's fair here. Can't you do that much?"

I made no promises. Partly because the identity of the murder weapon wasn't the only thing we knew. At this point, David satisfied the three classic criteria every killer possessed: means, motive, and opportunity. Richards had gambled away David's livelihood and left David saddled with at least half the responsibility for Richards' family, if Kemp's appeal was true. He'd been out on his snowmobile this morning when the crime occurred, which meant he had opportunity to commit the crime.

David might not be the killer, but Kemp should be looking at him pretty damn hard.

After bundling up again, gloves and hood in place, we exited the cruiser and trekked toward the wide porch overhang in front of Eagle Creek Cafe's door. About half-way across the parking lot, Kemp turned toward the road we'd just left and said, "Look. Look out there and tell me this place isn't beautiful."

I cast my gaze on Eagle Creek Cafe's surroundings. Evergreen trees, blue spruce, and hemlock pines were laden with heavy snow coating their branches like thick frosting. The never-ending snow, now that I'd accepted it as my constant cloying companion, did seem soft and lacy. Indeed, it was a gorgeous setting.

But I preferred open roads and sidewalks, Hillsborough Bay and palm trees. I wanted to go back to Tampa. I was beginning to feel like Dorothy Gale and I wished I possessed a pair of magic ruby slippers.

We started another trek through the heavy snow. As he had before, Kemp walked in front of me to clear a path. I followed a few feet behind, paying attention to the uneven terrain and struggling to keep my balance on the rough stones beneath the snowpack.

After we'd traveled a few yards, I raised my head and turned my body to look around. Across the gray darkness, floodlights dotted the landscape and perversely contributed to my night blindness. Still, I saw something strangely menacing. What was that? A snowmobile? I hadn't heard its engine, but it was less snow covered than George's Jeep or the silver Caddy. What was it doing way over there? Where was its rider? The snowmobile could belong to David Mason. In fact, the more I thought about it, the more likely it seemed.

The flat parking lot was better lit than the surrounding lawns. Outside the light halos, shadows swayed buffeted by the harsh gale. I squinted through the heavy snowfall, which didn't improve my weak distance vision any.

But I definitely saw something.

Two white tail deer? A couple of black bears? Or Mason with someone else?

They were too far from me and moving away and there was too much blinding snow. But they didn't look right. Call it instinct or whatever. I don't know. But it was damned odd.

Kemp had tromped ahead toward the entrance, breaking a trail.

"Justin!" I shouted, but the wind carried my voice in the opposite direction. He plowed onward, head down, focused on reaching his goal.

I looked again at the receding shadows across the distance. The two had separated slightly. Now they looked more like humans wearing parkas with huge hoods, similar to mine. But what the hell were they doing out there in the no-man's land between renovated grounds and hardwoods in this blizzard? Where could they possibly be going?

"Willa!" Kemp's voice came at me weakly as if from a wide distance, pulling my gaze from the shadows. "Willa! Come on!" He stood on the porch at the entrance door to Eagle Creek Cafe, waving me down the path he'd stomped moments before that was already filling with fresh drifts.

I waved back and pointed toward the shadows. By this time, they'd trudged far outside the light halos and deeper into the blinding blizzard. Kemp was fifty feet from where I stood. He probably couldn't see them at all.

As I watched, they moved into another light pool. The one cast by a stronger floodlight above the narrow wooden door that covered the entrance to the steam tunnels underneath the old hospital. The door was padlocked. Only the tour guide and the maintenance supervisor had keys, I'd been told when I took the tour years ago.

One of the shadows raised something heavy and bashed it down hard on the door. Then, he pushed the door open and he shoved the other shadow into the narrow opening and then followed and the door swung closed.

They were going down into the old steam tunnels. There was nothing down there but damp, cold, blackness. Spiders. Snakes. And dead critters of all sorts. I shuddered.

The tunnels stretched through the entire complex and once provided state-of-the-art steam heat for buildings that stretched out more than half a mile before the hospital was condemned years ago. The two shadows could walk from there through the tunnels into the main building. Maybe the snowmobile broke down. Maybe they simply wanted to get out of the blizzard for the rest of their travel.

But it didn't feel like that to me.

What made more sense is that they were headed in the opposite direction. Toward the new hospital and the parking garages. They could have driven there, too. So for whatever reason, they didn't want to be seen.

"Come on!" Kemp shouted, moving his left arm in a big arc as if he could herd me from the storm and into warm safety.

I mirrored the same gesture Kemp had made, guiding him my way before I turned, pulled off my oversized glove so I could fish out my cell phone and use the flashlight app to reveal the snow in front of me.

I began to trudge, raising each leg as high as I dared and carefully placing each heavy boot flat into the snow mound ahead, with deliberate speed.

Away from Kemp. Toward the tunnels..

CHAPTER EIGHTEEN

AFTER AN EXHAUSTING SLOG, I finally reached the green door. Heavy on its antique hinges, it rested open slightly. A thin ribbon of yellow light rimmed the edge, meaning the emergency bulbs burned inside.

A shiny silver padlock hung open on the rusty hasp. Maybe that meant a planned return through this exit instead of a one-way trip to a building or a different escape route.

Exertion and stress sweat trickled down from my armpits, clammy and cold.

I looked for Kemp behind me. He was taller, heftier and thus able to plow through faster than I had done. Still, he was fifty feet back.

The tunnels were warm and snow free.

"Kemp! I'm going down!" I shouted into the wind. He didn't hear me. I arced the app's flashlight beam a few times and hoped he glanced up to notice. Then I turned off the app and stowed the phone in my pocket. I pushed the green door as wide as I could and left it propped open by the snow bank before I ducked into the narrow stairway that led down into the tunnels.

Dank odors assaulted my nostrils. I pulled off the bulky gloves and stuffed them into my pockets and hurried as quickly as I dared in the huge boots down the narrow stone staircase, hanging onto both clammy side rails, deeper into the earth.

The tunnels were below basement level of the old building. Which meant maybe twenty feet or more below the surface. Emergency bulbs encased in metal baskets cast an eerie glow over the ancient bricks.

When I reached the bottom of the stairs and stepped a foot or two into the tunnel, balancing awkwardly on the sloped and slimy floor, I saw three travel options. Straight ahead east. Left north or right south.

Which way did the shadows go?

I heard my own heavy breathing, but no sounds from the two who had entered barely five minutes before.

No sound from Kemp behind me yet, either.

The east tunnel was short, maybe less than fifty feet ahead where it dead-ended under the front parlor of the building. There was no exit at that point, I remembered.

The north and south tunnels ran a quarter mile each in opposite directions. Exits once existed every one hundred feet or so, but several had been permanently closed.

The north tunnel led to the residences and a parking garage and, eventually, to the new hospital.

The south tunnel led to the basement of the Eagle Creek Cafe building. I couldn't remember how far away the exits were.

Which way did the two shadows travel? I could have called out to them. But should I have?

Before I could make a decision, someone turned the lights out. Instant total blackness. Which probably meant they'd found an exit and left me inside here. No worries. I'm not claustrophobic.

The green exit door was still unlocked. I could leave, trek outside in the blizzard the way I'd entered. All I needed to do was find the staircase and walk up.

But I couldn't see anything. At all. No ambient light of any kind. A wrong move in any direction could send me tumbling onto the cobblestone or worse. I could feel along the tunnel walls until I reached the opening, but my sense of direction was impaired by sensory deprivation, too. I wondered whether this was how a blind person felt navigating in the world.

I pushed my hand down into my pocket and patted around for my cell phone. When I pulled it out and pressed the home button, the screen lit up brighter than stadium lights. The battery was almost gone, but for now, until I could find the light switch, I could see.

I heard footsteps above and behind me. I turned and pointed my phone toward Kemp who had stopped when the lights went out. He'd been on his way down the stairs, gun drawn.

"There's no need for that, Justin. I'm fine. Whoever I followed in here must have left. Can you just reach back and flip—" the rest of my words were stolen by gunfire.

The first shot was true. It whizzed past my head and hit Justin square on the shoulder with enough force to knock him backward. He lost his footing and fell down the last three steps and banged his head soundly against the stone, which knocked him out cold.

His momentum pushed his body into me and I stumbled backward onto the slimy tunnel floor and dropped my phone. I scrambled over the slippery cobblestones to get to it before the screen light shut off and we were plunged into blackness again.

But Kemp had fallen right into my path.

I fumbled to crab over him, but before I reached across his slender torso, the screen shut off, plunging me into total darkness half a moment before the second gunshot whizzed past. I heard the ricochet and more hits before the noise stopped.

I rolled across Justin's body and slid to the opposite side, patting around the slimy rocks for my phone. When my hand bumped something soft and squishy a quick gasp escaped my mouth.

In the black silence my gasp doubled as a beacon for the third gunshot.

I clamped my lips together, hard, and forced my hands to feel along the disgusting tunnel floor, but patted nothing remotely like my phone.

Shit!

The fourth gunshot rang out and this one didn't bounce off the walls. It hit someone. I heard a man's groan followed by hard scrabbling grunts and groans that sounded like a struggle.

I could see nothing. The effect was surreal.

The fifth shot. An unmistakable human female scream was followed by total silence.

I counted silently, "One thousand one. One thousand two. One thousand three." I made it all the way to one thousand twenty eight before the emergency lights came back on.

I saw my phone had been mere inches from my hand and grabbed it. Kemp's gun was close, so I grabbed that, too. I pushed the power button on my phone and nothing happened. Maybe the battery drained or maybe the phone didn't survive the slam against the tunnel floor. Either way, the result was the same. No light. No nothing. *Dammit!*

Then I looked around wildly, prepared to duck again but

there was no wall to hide behind. Kemp groaned, perhaps returning to consciousness. His wound was bleeding profusely, adding to the slime.

I looked north and south, but the tunnel curved in each direction, cutting off my sight line. Was the gunman hiding around the corners? Or had he found an exit and already escaped?

In the east tunnel straight ahead, I saw the shadow that looked something like an apparition, but knew it had to be a person. Man or woman, I couldn't discern. Nor did it matter. Because it was holding the gun.

So I took a chance. The most logical option.

"Mason! Kemp's been shot!" I shouted, and immediately realized my voice was too loud. I lowered it a couple of notches. "David, I know what happened to Leo Richards." Which wasn't completely true. But I'd figured out enough to make a plausible guess. "He's been dead for months, hasn't he? His murder was staged today to make him look like a victim of the snow sniper. Did you kill him, David?"

I heard his ragged breathing. His deep voice confirmed my guesses. "No. I didn't."

"Who did kill Leo? Who's there with you?"

"I've been shot." He leaned against the tunnel wall and lowered the gun. "Get help, Willa. Before it's too late."

For a moment, I paused. Should I try to leave? He'd recognized me. Could David Mason be trusted not to shoot me when I stood up and became a bigger target?

"David, who is with you? How is she?"

Kemp needed help right away. For the woman, it might already be too late. She'd been completely silent. She could be unconscious. Or worse.

"Madeline Trevor. Ricochet hit." David's voice was breathless, weak.

"You mean it's Randy Trevor's wife?" I called back to confirm we were talking about the same person, which was a bit inane under the circumstances. I'd seen Madeline Trevor at the bridge club. She'd looked at me oddly, with what I now realized must have been suspicion. Maybe her husband had told her something about me. Or maybe she remembered me from back in the day. Either way, my presence must have pushed her over the edge.

"I don't know how bad," Mason said. "She planned to kill me. Leave me here." He seemed to have only enough wind to speak a few words each time. "I'd told her we'd had enough. She pulled a gun. She wanted to kill you. I tried to stop her. We struggled, but the gun went off. I didn't shoot at you, Willa. I swear." His voice was weaker with each short sentence.

Now that the emergency lights were on, I could see the steps leading to the green door and the blizzard, which all of a sudden seemed way less threatening than it had half an hour before. I checked Kemp's carotid pulse. Still beating. But he remained unconscious. No way could I get him up the steps.

"If I stand up, David, you're not going to shoot me, are you?" Not that I would trust his answer, but I wanted to keep him talking while I figured out what to do.

"Madeline shot at you. I didn't," he replied.

David slid down the tunnel wall and sat on the slimy floor. That decided me. No one would sit on that floor if they had a choice.

"I'm going for help. Don't move." I patted around in Kemp's pockets but didn't find his cell. "I need a phone. Mine's ruined. Do you have one?"

"Madeline does."

"I'm coming to get it. Don't shoot me." I walked gingerly over the slimy cobblestones, holding onto the tunnel wall to keep my balance. The last thing I needed was to fall again.

When I reached Madeline Trevor I checked for her carotid pulse, but found none. I patted her pockets until I found her phone, pulled it out of her pocket and dropped it into mine.

I turned to look at David Mason. He seemed to have passed out.

"I'll be right back. Kemp's a police officer. If he dies, you'll be in even bigger trouble than you already are. Stay put," I said. Would he do it? I didn't know. But I had to get help for Kemp. I had no choice.

I backed out of the tunnel, keeping a watch on Mason to be sure he didn't raise the gun. When I reached Kemp, I stepped over him, pulled myself up the steps, keeping as low a profile as I could, both hands on the rusty rails, until I burst into the night air. I ducked inside again and called down.

"David, I can see you from here. If you move, I'll turn off the light. You won't be able to get away in the dark." I flipped it off for a couple of seconds to prove I could and then flipped it back on. "Stay put."

No reply.

I reached into my pocket and pulled out Madeline's phone. When I pushed the button, her screen powered on and I almost whooped for joy. Until I saw the text notification that rested there.

I read it twice before the screen turned off. It was a text from her husband, Judge Randy Trevor. Only four words. "Is Mason dead yet?".

EPILOGUE

TWO DAYS LATER, GEORGE and I were once again seated at the back table at Eagle Creek Cafe, waiting for Marc Clayton. We'd taken a quick walk through the tunnels because George wanted to see where Madeline Trevor had died. The exit from the tunnels closest to the restaurant would have put her just inside the Cafe entrance. Her plan had been to leave Mason's body in the abandoned east tunnel and then return to the Cafe to complete her alibi. A plan that would have worked if I hadn't seen them across the parking lot that night.

Marc joined us, bringing hot coffee. "Sorry I'm late. I stopped off at the hospital to check on David Mason and Justin Kemp. They'll both recover. Kemp's shoulder surgery will take a little longer than David's abdominal wounds, though both of them will be able to return to work fairly soon."

"What about Randy Trevor?" George asked. He was still a bit angry about him and his wife. George is very protective of me and he takes a dim view of people trying to shoot me. Which I appreciate, of course.

"He's been transferred to jail in Grand Rapids for now," Marc said. "So, Willa, tell me what happened."

I leaned in and folded my hands around the warm coffee mug and wondered if I'd ever be warm again. "When we saw Leo Richards in his Toyota, his skin was unusually pink. I'd seen that before and heard testimony from medical examiners about it, but I couldn't recall the cause. It's similar to the cherry red hue bodies have when carbon monoxide poisoning is the cause of death. Pink *livor mortis* results when a body has been frozen."

"Ah," Marc said.

"When I remembered that, I knew that Richards was colder than he would have been if he'd simply been sitting after death in the Toyota in winter weather."

"Well, if he was already dead, why'd they shoot him in the head?" George wanted to know.

"To conceal the real cause of death."

"Which was what?" Marc asked.

"According to the statement the police took from Leo's wife, the cause of death was blunt trauma to the right temple. The bullet entered his left temple and destroyed the right side of his head with the exit wound. That obliterated most of the evidence that he'd been hit hard enough to kill him. A good forensic autopsy might still have found the real cause, but they had at least a fifty-fifty chance the coroner would miss it simply because the gunshot wound was substantial and sufficient." I explained the rest of the story as we finished our meal.

The whole thing had been a family affair.

There was a big fight fourteen months ago, as Kemp had originally told me. But what the sisters left out at the time was that during the fight, Madeline had killed Leo Richards. He'd been out of control in an argument with his wife and her sister had bashed his head in when she hit him too hard with a heavy bookend to stop him.

The three sisters hid the body in Maureen's basement chest freezer and concocted the disappearance story to cover up. Then they simply tried to carry on normally.

Until things began to fall apart.

When David discovered the extent of Leo's gambling losses and damage to the hardware business, David hired a private detective to find him. David's wife, the youngest sister Molly, begged him to stop looking for Leo, but David said he'd never, ever do that. That Leo needed to come back and face his responsibilities. So Molly told David about the murder to gain his cooperation.

Madeline was having trouble holding it together, too. Her behavior became so erratic that her husband, the judge, confronted her and she broke down and told him. Randy took control, which didn't surprise me in the least. He held everyone together to cover up the crime until the snow sniper came along and gave them all a chance to end the charade.

Randy knew about the impending arrest of the snow sniper. It was his idea to set up Richards' death as another snow sniper victim and to shoot Richards in the left temple to cause the exit wound to obliterate evidence of the blunt force trauma that had actually killed him. Madeline, Molly, and Maureen pulled off the setup and then attended the bridge club tournament to establish an alibi.

"Leo's wife, Maureen, gave a full confession this morning," I said, wrapping things up.

Marc pursed his lips and shook his head. George nodded. There was nothing more to say, really.

It was the pink skin that should have tipped me off to this

elaborate cover up. Leo Richards' body was too pink. I knew that pink came from being frozen and then thawed. But I missed it because the weather was so cold, I thought his body temperature was caused by the atmosphere. Turns out it was caused by his cold family.

George remained angry for a good long while, but his trademark sense of calm returned. We stayed to enjoy Pleasant Harbor for the full week and enjoyed a few of the cozy evenings we'd planned before we returned to Tampa.

I may not have owned a pair of ruby slippers and Madeline Trevor wasn't the Wicked Witch, but the entire episode reminded me that there's no place like home.

THE END

FALSE
JUSTICE

Thank you to some of the best readers in the world:
Beth Nagorsky (Desiree Rothchild), Phillip Mason, and
John Kuvacas (Antoine Crowe) for participating in our
character naming giveaways which make this book a bit
more personal and fun for all of us.

And for Wilhelmina Boersma, trailblazer extraordinaire.

CAST OF PRIMARY CHARACTERS

Judge Wilhelmina Carson
George Carson

Ursula Westfield
Desiree Rothchild
Antoine Crowe
Jason Taylor
Phillip Mason
Aaron Michaels

CHAPTER ONE

URSULA STEPPED INTO THE warm foyer of the restaurant at
precisely twenty to five and let out a long sigh of relief. It was
freezing in New York, and she'd been looking forward to
thawing out only to find it was uncharacteristically cold in
Tampa, barely topping out at forty degrees. She'd done her best
for the past couple of years to make sure her visits back home
had coincided with perfect, balmy weather, but on this particular
visit, the timing couldn't be helped.

She was glad for her coat as she'd made her way from the
parking lot into the building toward the hostess station where a
pretty young woman in a chic black sheath dress stood, teetering
on the stiletto heels of her knee-high black boots.

The grand old building, dubbed Minaret by its original
owner because of the silver dome on the top, was as magnificent
on the inside as it was on the outside. Across a private bridge
from Tampa's beautiful Bayshore Boulevard, Minaret sat on its
own private island, dubbed Plant Key, a sparkling jewel created
by dredging Hillsborough Bay more than a hundred years ago.

"Welcome to George's Place. I'm Desiree Rothchild. We're

happy to have you with us. Do you have a reservation this evening?"

Ursula ran a hand through her damp cap of dark hair and opened her mouth to reply, but her words were cut short by a booming voice.

"Ursula!" George Carson strode across the marble floor of the former ballroom toward her, a smile on his handsome face.

She pushed aside her rising apprehension over this visit and grinned with genuine pleasure. "George!" She stepped into the circle of George's outstretched arms for one of his patented bear hugs. He towered over her, even in her heels. "I'm so glad to see you."

"Willa said you'd called, but she wasn't sure if your flight out of JFK had been delayed." George stepped back and smiled. "Nasty weather up there. I'm sorry ours isn't a lot better tonight."

The ice storms that had been sweeping the Northeast all winter wreaked havoc on travel plans, but luckily, she'd sneaked out just before the latest front stacked up air traffic again. The scent of spicy tomato sauce and freshly baked bread wafted over her from a passing waiter, and she pulled back to give George's shoulder a squeeze, grateful for the momentary sense of comfort seeing him brought.

"I don't know what you guys have got cooking back there, but I can't wait to get some of it into my belly." She grinned. "I haven't had a great meal since I was here last."

She wasn't teasing. George's Place was the best restaurant in Tampa, even if he was too polite to brag. He'd won all of the culinary awards so many times that he'd been disqualified. The judges said keeping George's Place in the mix made competition impossible. Everything about the place was hard to match and impossible to beat, as far as Ursula was concerned.

George turned toward the hostess and held up two fingers. "Desiree, I'll put her at the booth in the alcove with the best view of the bay. We can move things around if you have to, okay?"

The young woman nodded as he snatched two menus from the hostess station and walked Ursula to her seat.

"Willa is tied up on a case until at least six, but she said she'll see you for drinks at the bar after your meeting. Sound good?"

"Can't wait. It's been way too long."

Wasn't that the truth? Her own career in broadcast journalism had exploded and, for the past year, her days started before sunup and didn't end until long after the moon was hanging high in the sky. Not that she was complaining. This was the culmination of everything she'd worked so hard for. Sometimes, though, she couldn't help but wonder if she'd spent all this time running, only to find the destination wasn't nearly as fulfilling as the journey.

She shoved the thought aside as George slowed to a stop next to a cozy booth with a stunning view, as promised. The water moved calmly, gleaming in the fading daylight. The palm trees that lined the shore looked almost out of place against the lackluster sky that had tucked its more brilliant, technicolor plumage away and offered up nothing more than a hint of burnt orange against gray smudge. To some, the sky might look ominous, but there was a stark sort of beauty in it that Ursula appreciated.

She made a mental note to break her own rule next year and bring Marcus here for the holidays. Willa and George hadn't met him yet, and she wanted him to see where she'd come from. She loved Tampa. She was sure Marcus would, too.

That settled, she unbelted her merino wool coat and slid it off her shoulders, flinging it onto the seat next to her before sitting.

"So how has that wife of yours been, George? Keeping out of trouble?"

George's hazel eyes went soft at the mention of his favorite person in the world, and he set the menus on the table.

"She's working a lot. Of course, we're both busy, as always." He swept a hand behind him toward the dining room, humming with activity that seemed excessive for a weekday so early in the evening. "Seems like I hardly see her. We appreciate the time we do have and make the most of it." He smiled again and shrugged. "It's a good life, Ursula. A *great* life. We've been lucky. I couldn't ask for more."

A waiter in a freshly pressed black and white uniform came by and stood off to the side, clearing his throat surreptitiously.

"Everything okay, Antoine?"

"Chef would like to speak with you in the kitchen when you have a moment. Something about the grouper shipment being short," he murmured in a low voice.

George sent Ursula an apologetic smile. "I'd hoped to sneak in a glass of wine with you before your dinner guest arrived, but apparently, I jinxed myself by bragging about how great everything is." He let out a good-natured laugh and backed away from the table before turning to the waiter. "Miss Westfield is a close family friend. Anything she needs, Antoine. Only the best." He smiled and clapped Antoine on the shoulder then stalked away to deal with his fish crisis before the big dinner rush.

Ursula ordered a glass of Cabernet and settled back into the buttery leather seat with a groan of relief. She was finally out of the freezing cold, and she hadn't been forced to come up with a lie to get George to leave her in privacy. Normally, she'd have loved to sit and chat with him, but until she got this meeting out of the way, she wouldn't be good company for anyone.

She thought back to the cryptic e-mail she'd received and chewed anxiously on her lower lip.

Federal Judge nominee Aaron Michaels is a murderer and I can prove it. Meet me at George's Place on December 12th at five p.m. Come alone and don't be late.

How many times over the past four days had she hemmed and hawed about showing up? Probably a thousand. But as much as she loved New York, Tampa was her hometown. The people here were *her* people. The thought that a man who was nominated to decide the fates of everyone who stepped into his courtroom was a *killer* had been too much to ignore.

Her friend, Judge Willa Carson, had told her that federal judges were appointed for life. It was nearly impossible to get one off the bench once he was appointed and confirmed. While Ursula figured that clear proof of murder should be plenty of cause to get rid of a federal judge, clear proof was hard to come by sometimes. The risk that a murderer would sit in judgment of others in her town was too high for her to be complacent about it.

She'd spent the rest of that first night furiously scouring the Internet and newsroom archives for anything and everything she could dig up about Aaron Michaels. What she'd found should've persuaded her to blow off this meeting.

A big, fat goose egg. The man was as clean as a whistle. In fact, she'd never had a deep-dive search like that come up so clean.

Michaels' story was as perfect as his hair. His square jaw fit for a super-hero. His wife and two perfect, Ivy League children so attractive, their public holiday card could've been stripped from an L.L. Bean catalog.

The judge Michaels was on tap to replace had died quite suddenly. Ursula wondered if her source planned to accuse Michaels of the man's murder, but after a few clicks, she found that he'd been suffering from a severe case of pneumonia that went awry. Natural causes, according to the official report.

Meaning squeaky clean Aaron Michaels was still squeaking.

And yet she couldn't shake a niggling sense that something felt off about him. Something in his eyes, maybe. Something she couldn't quite put her finger on had made her whip off a quick reply to her mysterious source. Yes, she would meet at George's Place, because she couldn't stand by if there was even a one percent chance this man was a killer.

Now here she was here in Tampa. Waiting.

There was a better than fifty percent chance she'd get stood up. That could be nothing more than the ramblings of a mentally ill person or a man with a grudge.

She almost hoped he wouldn't show. She'd have a great meal, a few drinks with Willa and George, lay a poinsettia on her mama's grave in the morning, and get the next flight back to New York with a clear conscience.

She'd barely completed the thought when a shadow fell over the table.

"Miss Westfield." The man's voice was low and raspy. She looked up with a start, daydreams of a pleasant, uneventful visit scattering like dandelion pods in the wind.

CHAPTER TWO

"YOU'RE EARLY," SHE SAID, gesturing to the seat across the table.

He was younger than she'd expected, mid-thirties. His tight, black curls were shorn close to his scalp, and his goatee was trimmed neatly like he'd just been to the barbershop. He slipped off his coat to reveal a dove gray suit, tailor-made for his fit physique. Dark, intelligent eyes searched her face as he slung his coat into the booth and folded his long legs under the table.

"Honestly, I didn't think you'd show." His gaze flicked nervously around the room before returning to meet hers.

"I almost didn't." She lowered her voice. "Your message was both disturbing and vague. You'd be surprised how many false accusations I get every day, but..."

"But?" He placed his briefcase on the seat next to him and kept a protective hand on it.

She shrugged. "I just had a gut feeling that I should hear you out. Prove me right, Mr.—?"

They both went silent as Antoine placed her wine on the table. He offered the man across from her a drink, but he declined. When they were alone again, he leaned closer.

"I'm sorry," he murmured, "but I'd rather not give you my name."

"You want me to investigate a story. Knowing your name would build some trust between us." She had to admit there was some kind of story here, though. He'd showed up, and he seemed to be lucid and intelligent enough. He didn't seem some nutter holding onto a conspiracy theory or a man bent on revenge. So far.

"I don't need you to investigate." His voice was slow, quiet. Almost a whisper, but not quite. Which made him hard to hear.

"And why is that?"

"Because I have proof."

Ursula leaned back against the seat and struggled to keep her face impassive. She'd been in broadcast journalism a long time.

Just because he looked normal didn't mean he was. The ones who looked normal were too often the ones you had to be most careful about. But the earnest expression on his face, the heat of truth burning in his eyes, made her blood run cold. Whatever he thought he had on Michaels, at least he believed it to be true.

He unfastened his leather briefcase and pulled out a manila folder. For a moment, he seemed to hesitate. Then, with one more surreptitious glance around the room, he slid the folder across the table. She let it lie there.

"I have the original in my briefcase. This copy is for you." He tapped the folder with two fingers.

She called on the steely determination that had served her so well in her field all these years and flipped open the folder.

The image that stared back at her hit her like a physical blow to the stomach. A gasp had puffed from her lips before she clamped them shut and swallowed hard.

She'd seen her share of heartbreaking crime scenes and photos. No way to avoid it in her line of work.

This one was hard to look at.

It was a full body shot of a woman standing upright. Mottled bruises marred her light brown skin. Her slim neck was bisected by an angry welt that raised from the rest of her skin.

Even in the grainy image, which must have been snapped hours after her attack, it was clear to see she'd suffered. But it was her face that had Ursula's throat aching.

The woman gazed into the camera, brown eyes empty, head bowed. Dead inside but left alive. Beaten in every sense of the word.

The wine Ursula sipped threatened to come back up and she pursed her lips tighter until she regained her composure.

"You're saying Michaels did this?" she finally managed, after a long pause.

The man nodded. "He did."

"And then he murdered her?"

He broke eye contact then and stared down at the gleaming silver flatware on the table before him. "Maybe he didn't pull the trigger, but he might as well have. After the rape, she couldn't take the nightmares and constant fear." His voice shook with conviction. "He drove her to it."

Ursula weighed her words carefully. "Did she go to the police at the time?"

His jaw clenched, and he busied himself, buckling his briefcase, refusing to meet her gaze. "No."

"Please don't take this the wrong way, but it's crucial. Why didn't she report this?"

"He threatened her. She was nobody." His mouth twisted into a grim smile. "Thirty years ago. A brown girl trying to pay her way through school by working at one of the fancy country clubs. And he was an Ivy Leaguer with a daddy in politics and a bright future. You do the math."

His face was a mask of pain. A surge of pity pulsed through her, and she instinctively reached for his hand in a gesture meant to comfort.

"I'm so sorry she suffered this. But I'm not sure what I can do to help. The crime is decades old, and without proof that Michaels was the one responsible, I—"

He jerked his hand away and lurched to his feet, dark eyes blazing.

"I know all that," he said, harshly. "I know it's probably too late for her."

He leaned toward her. His voice dropped to a near-whisper that was no less intense. "But men like this? They don't just stop and magically turn into model citizens." He stabbed the folder with two fingers. "That woman was my mother. He did this to her. And he's done worse to others."

Ursula's stomach lurched. "You have proof he's done this again?"

"He takes what he wants and damn the cost. He's on the shortlist of candidates and, the word is, it's looking good for him. You want a man capable of this," he stabbed the file folder again, "do nothing. Otherwise, do your job. Make sure the world knows who he really is."

She reached out and grabbed his wrist. "Tell me your mother's name. I can't do anything unless I know her name."

He shook her grip from his arm. "I've given you the proof. The rest is up to you." He left the folder on the table between them and stalked away.

Ursula stared after him, still shaking when she heard her name.

"Ursula!" She turned to see George winding through the diners toward her table.

Quickly, she shoved the picture back into the folder and slid it into her oversized purse.

"Willa arrived a few minutes ago," he said as he approached. "She's in the Sunset Bar armed with a bottle of 1964 Bertani Amarone she's been saving until you came to visit. Come on."

"Excellent," she said, weakly. She collected her belongings and realized that the man had left his coat. She picked it up. "Let me give this to Desiree. He might come back for it."

George took the coat from her. "Maybe Desiree can catch him. You go ahead. I'll join you later. We're overbooked in here tonight. Don't wait for me to open that wine."

She nodded as he hurried away. She hated that her conversation with the man had ended so abruptly. Once she sorted it all out, she'd try to e-mail him again. But the crime was thirty years old. He could wait until tomorrow.

She threaded the crowd toward Willa, but her mind was a million miles away. On the woman in that photo and the man who'd allegedly hurt her.

Her instincts had predicted the story was going to be bad. And now that she'd seen that photo, she could never unsee it. It was burned behind her eyelids as she let them drift briefly shut.

In that moment, prudent or not, she decided to get that woman justice, or die trying. And she knew precisely who could help her make good on her promise.

She returned Willa's delighted wave and hustled a little faster toward that wine.

CHAPTER THREE

"WELL, IF IT ISN'T the big-time New York television star."
Willa grinned as Ursula approached, green eyes sparkling, and
then slid from her barstool to pull her in for a hug. "As I live and
breathe."

Ursula returned the embrace and then drew back, trying her
best to remember what it felt like to act normal. "Not exactly a
star. Just a hard-working reporter. Same as always."

She followed Willa to a quiet corner of the Sunset Bar and
slid a glass half full of ruby red liquid a little closer to her.
"Always the soul of modesty. Now tell me about that new man.
I've been dying to meet him. Marcus, right?"

She nodded and toyed with the stem of her glass. "I'd like to
bring him here soon to meet you guys."

"We'd be delighted." Willa cocked her head, her keen
eyes searching Ursula's face for a long moment. "What's
up?"

The worry line between her brows creased, a beacon that
something serious was on her mind. She wouldn't burden Willa
with the sad tale yet. Especially when her colleague's reputation

was on the line and Ursula had nothing but an accusation to work with. So far.

She forced a smile and shook her head again. "I'm just a little tired, really. But tell me how are Harry and Bess?"

Willa was crazy for her Labrador retrievers, and the question got a grin out of her. "Spoiled rotten, if you must know. George has taken to bringing them scraps of filet mignon from the kitchen on the weekends. Now they turn their noses up at their kibble and we have to run an extra two miles every day to get rid of the calories."

"Lucky dogs," Ursula said, pausing to take a sip of the pricey wine. "Oh my, is that good."

"It certainly is," Willa said, practically smacking her lips. "How about a cheese plate to go with it? George has a few wonderful bleus on the menu."

The thought of eating now made her stomach pitch, but she nodded anyway. "Sure, sounds good. So what else? How is the job going?" She kept her tone light, but she was hoping for inside information on Aaron Michaels. "Anything new in the world of criminal justice?"

"Same old, same old. Actually, it's kind of nice for a change. I love the work, but it's been blissfully dull lately. Let's drink to no drama for the rest of the year." She held up her glass, and Ursula followed suit. They clinked the crystal goblets together before sipping.

No drama, indeed. Ursula shoved aside the guilt and cleared her throat. "I heard something about a new federal judicial appointment in your district. A couple of state court judges on the short list, according to the scuttlebutt. One of them from Tampa. Aaron Michaels? You know him?"

"Not well, but yes." Willa's eyes narrowed, and she gazed at

Ursula with what felt like the same look she gave criminal defendants. "I've met him once or twice at meetings and charity events. Why do you ask?"

Ursula shrugged. Willa was too smart to fool for long, and her antenna was clearly twitched. "The network wants a human-interest piece—you know, making the public familiar with him."

No such story existed yet. But it would. One way or another. And if the story was good enough, the network would want it. So she wasn't lying to a federal judge. At least, not exactly.

Willa swirled the wine in front of her, considering it for a moment. "Well, I don't know too much about h—"

The rest of Willa's sentence was cut off by a terrified scream just outside the window.

Ursula reeled around, straining to see through the beveled glass, but in the next instant the door to the restaurant swung open and a woman rushed in, screeching for someone, *anyone,* to call nine-one-one.

Her face was white and her whole body was shaking.

George rushed to the foyer from one of the dining rooms. He leaned toward Desiree, presumably telling her to make the call. He stepped up to the woman, hand outstretched. "Are you all right? Are you hurt?"

"Not me, not me." She shook her head rapidly and then pointed out the door. "The man. I don't—I don't know what happened. I was just walking and he…"

Her voice broke on a sob as George led her outside. Willa stood to follow, and Ursula went after her.

A knot of premonition formed in Ursula's stomach as they moved into the chilly night air. George was bent over a prone figure on the ground.

The woman's shrill voice blathered, "I was just walking past, and there he was. Lying there, right in front of me. I don't know what happened. Is there a doctor in there?" She shot a panicked glance over her shoulder toward the restaurant. "There has to be a doctor somewhere!"

The blood rushed in Ursula's ears as she took another step closer, craning her neck to see past George's wide shoulders. When she finally had a clear view of the body on the ground, her heart skittered to a stop.

The man she'd been speaking with only minutes before was lying on the pavement. He stared unseeingly up at the sky, the life fading from his eyes as blood pooled around him.

George knelt beside him.

"It's too late for a doctor," Willa said softly, her legendary grace under fire in full effect as she drew the now sobbing woman away from the body. She and George exchanged glances as she led the woman toward the restaurant's entrance.

"Looks like he's been stabbed several times. At least once in the kidney," George said, barely audible over the voices of diners and staff rushing out of the restaurant. George was always calm and collected under any circumstances. His very reliability often infuriated his wife. But tonight, Ursula found him reassuring.

Dark red blood seeped from a deep gash in the man's side, and the front of his gray suit had blossomed with a wide, scarlet stain before his heart stopped pumping.

Ursula's mind raced as action exploded around them. A woman came outside and identified herself as a doctor and dropped to her knees beside his prone body, but it was all background noise. A small knot of diners had spilled outside. Sirens in the distance grew louder. She glanced toward Bayshore Boulevard and saw police and rescue vehicles speeding toward the Plant Key Bridge. They'd be on the island shortly.

As the doctor worked, and George ushered his guests back inside, Ursula looked on in disbelief. Her gaze skimmed over the scene. Nearly everything about the young man looked the same. Except for his briefcase. His briefcase was gone.

Willa returned outside and stood next to Ursula. Her gaze was troubled as she looked down at the man.

"Have you ever had a mugging here on your island before?" Ursula asked.

"Too much effort for too little reward. Muggers usually rob their victims." Willa shook her head. "But diners here rarely carry cash. What would a garden-variety mugger hope to gain?"

CHAPTER FOUR

FIRST RESPONDERS ARRIVED MOMENTS later and went to work, scattering in an organized form of chaos. The lead officer talked quietly with George. The medical team triaged the victim and loaded him into the ambulance, closed the doors and sped across the bridge toward Tampa Southern Hospital.

After the body was removed, Willa touched her arm. "Thank you for not making an immediate media circus out of this Ursula. Let's go back inside. They'll come find us."

When they were settled into their seats again with coffee instead of wine, Willa said, "Okay. Who was that guy and what were you two talking about?"

Ursula blinked, taken aback. She cocked her head, "What do you mean?"

Willa's eyes narrowed. "I saw you with him when I first came in. That's why I didn't join you right away."

"He is—was—a confidential source for a story." Ursula wouldn't lie to Willa. And anyway, what would be the point? The man was dead, and she didn't even know his name, let alone whether anything he'd told her was true.

Willa rested her forearms on the table and leaned forward. "What kind of story? About Judge Michaels?"

Ursula paused, thinking about where to go from here. What did she really know for certain? Not much. Willa wasn't a competitor seeking to scoop her story. And she'd want to keep a corrupt judge off the bench just as much, or more, than Ursula did.

"Yes, Judge Michaels." She nodded and took a deep breath. "He'd sent me an e-mail and asked to meet with me. Something about his claims pushed my buttons, I guess. Or maybe I just wanted an excuse to come home for a couple of days."

"This could be important, Ursula. Maybe even related to his murder." Willa leaned in, frowning. "What did he say to you?"

She hesitated. If she told Willa about the man's accusations—hell, even if she showed the picture—without more, would his unverified claims make any difference? Probably not.

Could she find a way to verify his claims? Again, probably not. The rape victim was long dead, and the statute of limitations expired years ago. And even if the old case was somehow still viable, the dead man had admitted there was no evidence at all to tie the judge to the crime. No rape kit, no police report, not even a diary entry.

Still, it was her job to report the news. Verified allegations that Aaron Michaels was unfit to be a federal judge would be big news that might actually make a difference. Finding the killer of a man murdered in a parking lot was a job for the police.

Ursula squared her shoulders. "He didn't tell me his name. He showed me this old photograph."

She reached into her purse and grabbed the photo in its

folder. She pushed the folder across the table to Willa. "He gave me this for evidence."

Willa flipped the folder open and studied the grainy picture, her face impassive. She'd seen worse in her courtroom, and she'd long ago schooled herself against showing the emotions Ursula was sure she must be feeling.

Ursula continued. "He said Judge Michaels was responsible for beating this woman. That he'd raped her. And that he got away with it. He claimed that the rape drove her to suicide."

Willa closed the folder and looked up. "Is that everything he said?"

"Yes." Ursula paused and took another breath. "But I think the woman was his mother."

"I see." Willa folded her hands on the table. "That's not all, is it?"

Ursula shook her head. "He had a briefcase when he was talking to me. He had copies of this photo inside, and I don't know what else. I didn't see the briefcase near his body outside."

Willa nodded. She sipped her coffee, thinking. "The police will take a statement from you tonight. It's a crime to lie to police during an active homicide investigation, Ursula. You know that."

"And you know that if I tell his story now, it'll become part of the police report and be all over the news. The claims are too salacious for some of my less ethical competitors to ignore. I don't know that any of what that man said is true. Revealing everything would damage Judge Michaels' reputation at a critical time in his career, based on nothing but a photo and accusations." Ursula shook her head and frowned. "That doesn't sit well with me. Surely, you don't think I should be a part of character assassination like that, do you?

With absolutely no proof of any kind? Not even a second source?"

Before Willa could reply, a slouched and haggard looking Tampa Police Department plain clothes detective with a badge clipped to his belt approached them.

"I'm Detective Phil Mason." His voice was deep and sonorous, but his expression brooked no argument. "Judge Carson, I have a few questions for Miss Westfield."

Willa nodded. "Of course."

Ursula pursed her lips and collected the manila file folder from the table and stuffed it into her purse before turning to face the detective again. "Lead the way."

She followed Mason through one dining room, then another, until finally, they reached a little office in the back beside the fire exit. From there, she heard the clinking of pans, chefs swearing at their prep cooks, and the gentle sizzle of the burners.

The noise might have been enough to irritate her another time, but now she was all too grateful for the din. Any excuse to focus on something else was a welcome one.

"Sorry for the cramped quarters." Mason settled himself behind what Ursula assumed was the manager's desk, and she took a chair opposite him, folding her hands in her lap in front of her.

"That's okay. Good to know the world still spins." She tilted her head toward the noisy kitchen.

"Right." Mason's hangdog expression became more pronounced as his blond eyebrows pulled low over his sunken, tired eyes. "Well, first things first, I suppose. As I said, I'm Detective Phil Mason." He gave her a card and asked for her ID, jotting notes as they spoke.

"So, as I understand it, you met with Mr. Taylor shortly

before the incident this evening?" Detective Mason asked though he didn't look up from his notebook.

Mr. Taylor. She tucked the name away and nodded. "We didn't speak for very long," Ursula hedged, holding her purse tightly closed on her lap.

"And what was the nature of your conversation?"

"Well…not much, really. He had e-mailed me letting me know about a possible news story. But when we met tonight, he seemed twitchy. Nervous. He didn't say much of anything before running off."

The detective looked up. "There was no mention of what he wanted to tell you in his initial e-mail?"

"I imagine if he could have e-mailed the information, he would have. Besides, I'm sure you know how people are when they're being interviewed. They get nervous." As if to prove her point, she wrung her hands tighter around her purse in her lap.

Detective Mason's mouth contorted slightly into what might have been a sympathetic smile. "I see."

"He didn't even tell me his name." Ursula nodded, nervously. "He had a briefcase with him, though. And when I saw him, uh, afterward, in the parking lot? I didn't see the briefcase."

The Detective glanced at her bag, and for a brief, insane moment, Ursula felt like he could see inside it, could see the contents that she was determined to keep secret until she could prove a connection to Judge Michaels.

Don't ask me anything else. Just let me go.

He flipped to a new page in his notebook. "What did the briefcase look like?"

She closed her eyes to visualize what she'd seen only for a couple of seconds. "It was kind of medium brown leather. It had a flap and buckles on the front." She gestured over her shoulder. "A long strap."

"Was it monogrammed?"

She thought about it and shook her head. "I didn't see a monogram."

He nodded and finished his note. "Anything else you can recall about Mr. Taylor?"

"He dashed out so quickly that he left his coat in the booth where we were sitting. I gave it to George, and he gave it to Desiree, the hostess."

Mason made a note of that, too. "Anything else?"

She shook her head again. *Just let me go. Just let me go.*

"Okay. Thanks for your time. I'll call you for a follow-up in a few days if we need to." Mason closed his notebook and stuffed it into his pocket along with his pen. "Something might come back to you. If it does, you'll let me know?"

She gave him a shaky nod. "Of course. You have my card. Call anytime."

If the police found the briefcase, they'd have copies of the photo, and whatever else he had in there. While they looked for the briefcase, she planned to look for something, anything, to confirm what Taylor had told her about Michaels.

She returned to the restaurant, but Willa had gone. She sat at the bar and ordered another glass of wine because the one she'd left when she ran out to the parking lot had disappeared. She reassured herself that she had, in fact, made the right decision. For now.

Tomorrow morning, she'd do what she did best. Find another source to support Taylor's story.

CHAPTER FIVE

THE NEXT DAY, URSULA sat on the too-firm mattress in her hotel room, listening to the whirr of the ice machine down the hall while flipping through one web page after another. Experience told her that a man who abused one woman was likely to have been abusive to other women. If Taylor was right about Aaron Michaels attacking his mother, there were probably more victims.

The thing was, she had not found even a smidge of scandal, nor a whiff of wrongdoing by Judge Michaels. Nothing in his past and nothing in the present, either.

Her online investigation of the judge had turned up all the same things it had before she arrived in Tampa—a family full of beautiful kids, all perfectly balanced and successful. A wife whose smile was so toothy and white that she might have been auditioning for a toothpaste commercial. And, of course, the judge himself.

Article after article detailed his contributions to charities in the Tampa area, his tough but fair rulings, and his personal volunteering for community outreach programs. It was like the guy was prepping for sainthood.

Which really triggered Ursula's radar. No man was that clean. And especially not a judge. Judges made enemies simply by doing their jobs well. Yet, she uncovered not one negative word against Michaels.

She rubbed the back of her neck and stretched her sore shoulders. She'd been hunched over the computer too long. But she did manage to unearth a few noteworthy points.

Judge Michaels had not been in Tampa the previous evening. Or in Florida at all.

No, he was off spreading his benevolence around at a hundred-dollar-a-plate charity ball in D.C. alongside his ex-debutant wife and their eldest son.

Good for him. He had an alibi—he hadn't killed Taylor. Or at least, he hadn't done the deed himself. Which made her feel slightly better about what she'd left out of her statement to Detective Mason.

But his alibi didn't prove he was not involved in Taylor's murder.

She clicked over to the judge's website again and stared at the phone number. A direct line to his office. She could simply call to make an appointment. Or she could go over to the courthouse. It was a public building, after all.

But she couldn't confront him today because he wasn't there. Besides that, what would she confront him with? Unsupported charges from a dead man who could never speak out against him?

She clicked back to the list of events in D.C. to confirm that he was scheduled to speak at the event today and again tomorrow as well. Which meant he wouldn't return to Tampa for at least another forty-eight hours.

Squaring her shoulders, she dialed the judge's office number and maneuvered through the directory of choices until she reached the desk she wanted.

The phone rang twice and then a steely, serious female voice answered. "Judge Aaron Michaels' office, how can I help you?"

"Hi, this is Ursula Westfield. I'm with Judicial World News, and I was hoping to do a short piece on the judge while I'm in the area, because he's on the short list for the federal judgeship. Is he available at all tomorrow?"

"I'm afraid he is not. Perhaps if you try again next—"

"Actually, I can't. I'm only in town for the next two days," Ursula rushed, then, taking a deep breath, she added, "Is there anyone else I might be able to speak with instead? It's going to be a great piece about his charity work and whatnot, but I could use a personal anecdote or quote."

Silence punctuated the air. Ursula gritted her teeth, wondering if she'd somehow come on too strong, too suspicious. But then, the woman on the other line spoke.

"Well, I can ask him if he calls in."

"What about his law clerk? She might be able to help me." Ursula's experience with law clerks was that they were loyal to their judges. She'd get nothing negative from the clerk, but she just wanted to get into the office. Look around. Find something she could use. She knew it was a long shot, but nothing else had panned out. If she didn't make any progress by the end of the day, she'd go back to New York empty-handed.

"I'll ask her to pick up. Hold on, please," the woman said.

Another brief pause, and then the woman came back. "She has an opening for three o'clock on her schedule."

"Perfect." Hope, sure and solid, swelled in her chest. "And what is her name?"

"Tiffany Strong. I'll let her know to expect you, and the

security desk will be able to direct you when you get here. Have a good evening." The line clicked off.

She searched out everything she could find about Tiffany Strong. By all accounts, she was as pristine as the judge himself.

She'd gone to a reputable school and received respectable grades. She'd interned in several different law offices during law school before finally coming to work with the judge. Even her posts on social media were sterile.

She had friends, a boyfriend, and hobbies, but none of that clogged her social media feeds. No selfies with her half-drunk friends and no pictures of her making out with her boyfriend. There were only photos of her smiling at the camera, usually holding an award or her pet cat, with her blond hair perfectly in place and not a single blemish on her smooth, youthful face.

Hopefully in this case youth went hand in hand with gullibility because she was going to be pressing poor Tiffany pretty hard and could really use a break of some kind.

Ursula closed her laptop and slid it into the bag beside her bed before she popped into the shower.

CHAPTER SIX

WHEN URSULA KNOCKED ON Tiffany Strong's office door
at three o'clock, she was no better informed than she had been
the night before. Tiffany had spent three years of her career
working closely with Judge Michaels. If there were something
dark and twisted about him, she'd likely have seen at least a
glimpse of it at one point or another. The trick now was to get
something useful from her.

The door swung open, and the pretty, blond woman she'd
seen in countless photos smiled up at her. She was shorter than
Ursula had expected, and thinner, too, but her poise and air of
total competence were exactly as advertised.

"Come in," Tiffany swept her hand out, then stuck it in front
of Ursula. "Pleasure to meet you, Ms. Westfield."

"Call me Ursula, please." Ursula shook hands and then sank
into one of the worn green leather wingback chairs opposite her
desk. State court law clerks didn't have a huge budget or palatial
offices. If Judge Michaels moved onto the federal bench, all of
that would change for him. For Tiffany, too, if he took her along
to the federal courthouse.

Tiffany settled into her desk chair, still grinning broadly, and then said, "What can I help you with? I was told you wanted to put a personal touch on a human-interest story about the judge?"

Ursula glanced around the office briefly. The walls were lined with filing cabinets and bookshelves stacked with leather-bound books meant to impress. Legal research was done by computer these days. Several picture frames held the originals of the photos Ursula had seen online—Tiffany's graduation day, her mewling cat, and then one of Tiffany alongside her boss at a local bar association dinner last year.

"He's got quite the career, doesn't he? And maybe the nomination now. You must be thrilled."

"We're cautiously optimistic." Tiffany's grin broadened.

Ursula cleared her throat. "So, you and the judge have worked together for nearly three years, is that right?"

She nodded, practically beaming, like a mother with a new baby. "I was an intern and then assisted his previous clerk before taking over my current position last year."

"What can you tell me about him as a man? If you had to pick his best quality, say."

Tiffany reflected on this, and for a moment her thin face took on an almost dreamy expression before she schooled her features into a polite smile. She glanced at the picture of herself with the judge. "I'm not sure I know where to start. Aaron is…the judge, I mean, he's truly remarkable. Like no man I've ever known, frankly."

"Is that right? How so?" Ursula raised her eyebrows.

"He's a great father. And husband," Tiffany said, almost perfunctorily.

"I've read that about him," Ursula nodded. "But he's neither of those things to you. What's your personal experience with him?"

Tiffany's gaze swept over her, appraising, and Ursula resisted the urge to straighten her hair or something.

"Well, he's considerate," Tiffany finally said, choosing her words carefully. "I remember one time my car broke down. It was my first week working here, and I was so nervous about being late. But when I called to tell him what happened, he just couldn't have been nicer. He even came and looked at my car himself. He wound up ruining his suit, but he fixed the darn thing."

"So a real knight in shining armor," Ursula murmured as she scribbled in her notebook, but her gaze never left Tiffany. The younger woman was wringing her hands in her lap, her eyes flicking to the photo on her bookshelf every few minutes.

"He really is. He's taught me so much. Not just about law, either. He's...well, my life wouldn't be the same without him." Again, slavish devotion crossed Tiffany's face, and Ursula frowned, wondering how best to approach her suspicions.

"Would you say you're very close with the judge and his family?" Ursula lifted an eyebrow, and Tiffany's cheeks reddened slightly.

"He's been my boss for a long time, I mean you have to sort of know someone quite well by that point."

"And are you aware of any accusations of misconduct leveled against the judge?" she said the words lightly, but Tiffany's stiffened instantly.

"Of course not. Not at all."

But the look on her face said she did know.

Adrenaline shot through Ursula as silence settled over the room.

This was the precipice right here. Either she went for it, or she backed off. Tiffany knew something. She was sure of it.

But if she asked outright, her cover story about a puff piece was blown, and Tiffany might call security. She weighed the risks and sucked in a breath. *No guts, no glory.*

"Look, Tiffany, this...this is off the record." Ursula placed her notebook inside her bag and then met the younger woman's eyes as she leaned in. "I like Judge Michaels. I think he's the best man for the job. I'm here to warn you about some rumors floating around."

"I don't know what you mean." But the look on her face clearly said otherwise. "Please leave. Now."

Ursula sat up straighter. "Are you having an affair with Judge Michaels? Is that why you don't want to talk to me?"

"Absolutely not. That's ludicrous. Where did you hear that?" Fiery indignation coated every word and Ursula's pity for the woman ratcheted up another notch.

She wouldn't be the first young woman to be taken in by a powerful, married man.

"You need to see this." Ursula pulled the manila envelope from her bag, careful to hide the notes she'd scribbled on the front, then slid the photo out and toward Tiffany.

"What's this?" She barely glanced at the picture and rolled her eyes. "Ancient history."

Ursula's throat went dry. "W-what do you mean?"

"I've heard the rumors. We all did a while back. He supposedly got rough with a prostitute?" She guffawed. "This is what people do. They take a great man like Aaron, and they try to doctor up some crap story like he's a villain because they want someone else for the job. Fake news, that's all it is. You of all people should know that rumors are exactly that—rumors.

Nothing more." She lifted the photo and tossed it across the desk. "Now I believe I asked you to leave."

"But—"

"*Leave*," Tiffany pushed the word through gritted teeth. "I won't have you talking about Aaron like this. If you continue to harass us or disclose those photos to anyone, I will have you arrested. Blackmail is a crime in this state, Ms. Westfield. Bury those doctored pictures wherever you found them. Now get out before I call the bailiff."

Defiance shone in Tiffany's eyes, and somehow, despite everything Ursula had uncovered so far, Tiffany's anger was one of the most unnerving parts of this story. Tiffany wasn't simply in denial about Judge Michaels. She wouldn't even glance at the photos because she didn't care about the truth. All she wanted was to keep her distorted image of Aaron Michaels intact.

And maybe, just maybe, she would be willing to kill in order to defend it.

"Right." Ursula nodded, and then shoved the picture back into her purse. She rose slowly and walked to the door. "Thank you for your time, Ms. Strong."

CHAPTER SEVEN

URSULA STARED AT THE image of the young woman on the screen, a heavy sadness closing over her. *Millie Taylor.*

This picture was much better than the one she'd seen of the girl at George's Place last night. Here, a young Millie was smiling for her class yearbook. A smile that held so much hope. Unless Ursula's instincts failed her, Millie's bright future had been stripped away just a couple years later by Aaron Michaels.

Ursula shifted on the desk chair and straightened her aching back. It had been a long day and was setting up to be an even longer night. Once the police had released the name of the man who had been murdered in front of the restaurant—Jason Taylor—it had been easy enough to find out about his mother.

What was taking much longer was trying to find anyone willing to talk honestly, on the record, about Michaels. She'd hit one roadblock after another, and, eventually, she'd thrown her net far and wide. If he didn't know she was investigating him already, he'd know soon enough. Probably the day after tomorrow when he got back to town.

Which meant there was no time for rest, and there was even

less time to be a yellow-bellied chicken. It was time to get help.

She tapped her fingernails on the screen of her phone for a second before punching up a contact number. She held the phone to her ear and waited as it rang.

"Hey, Ursula," Willa said. "Are you still in town?"

Willa's voice made Ursula prickle with interest. "Yes. Why?" Another call came in. She looked at the phone. Detective Mason. "Willa, can I call you right back?"

"Of course."

"Thanks." Ursula hung up and took Mason's call. "Ursula Westfield here."

"Ms. Westfield, we've located Jason Taylor's briefcase. We also got a warrant for his e-mails. Interesting reading." Mason paused, perhaps believing she would blurt out something foolish. When she didn't, he said, "You weren't his only pen pal, Ms. Westfield. I'm calling to tell you to be careful."

"What do you mean?"

"Mr. Taylor was targeted first, then followed, and then murdered. The killer probably knows you were there. Knows what you know." He paused. "Might be a good idea for you to get out of town until we wrap this thing up."

Her mouth dried up. She felt her heart pounding. "I don't know much of anything. I'd have told you."

"That's not exactly true, is it? You know that Jason Taylor believed Aaron Michaels was a rapist and drove his mother to kill herself."

Now her pulse was throbbing in her ears so loudly she could barely hear. She cleared her throat. "He had no proof of that. None at all. And it was a long time ago. If I'd told you about it, are you saying you would have investigated the old crime?"

"No. We wouldn't have. You're right about that." Someone

called Mason's name in the distance. "I've gotta go. Be careful, Ms. Westfield. Better yet, be on the next plane to New York tonight. Come back after we catch Taylor's killer."

Ursula sank onto the bed. Her hands were shaking, and her thumb accidently hit the redial button on the last call she'd made.

Willa picked up again. "That was fast."

Ursula pressed the speaker button. "Detective Mason found Jason Taylor's briefcase. He knows about the photos. About Millie Taylor. He's read our e-mail exchanges." Her voice was as shaky as her hands.

"Yes, and that's not all." Willa took a sip of something. "Why don't you come over here for dinner. I'll tell you what I've found out about Aaron Michaels."

"You've been looking into Michaels?"

"I told you things were dull at work." Ursula heard the smile in Willa's voice before she spoke seriously again. "Based on what you told me last night, and what I know of your work, I had no doubt you were on to something. So I poked around with my contacts a little and a couple of interesting things popped up." Willa paused. "Do you want to know, or not?"

Ursula rubbed at her temples to stave off an oncoming headache. "I don't want this to blow back on you. He could be one of your colleagues soon."

Both women went quiet at the chilling thought.

"Don't worry about me," Willa said, finally. "I can handle myself. And George is here. But you shouldn't be alone. Are you coming over?"

"Yeah. Let me get a quick shower. I feel grimy." She glanced at the clock. It was still early. This day seemed to have lasted way too long already. "Thanks so much. And Willa? I apologize again."

"No need. Bring an umbrella and dress warmly. That cold front has brought some icy rain down from Canada. Talk soon." Willa disconnected.

Ursula set the phone down. She stepped into the bathroom and turned on the shower. She rummaged around in her carry on for makeup remover and shampoo. She was about to slip into the hot shower when her hotel room phone rang.

The front desk, maybe? She sat on the bed and picked up the receiver. "Hello?"

"Ms. Westfield?"

The words were timid, almost a whisper.

She was about to catch a break. She could almost smell it. Ursula sat perfectly still as if the simple act of breathing might scare the woman off. She schooled herself to sound calm and controlled. "Yes, this is she."

"Tiffany Stone told me about you. I have something about Judge Michaels you'll want to see," the tinny, female voice said. "Something important. Can we meet somewhere and talk?"

The woman sounded young. She also sounded terrified. Ursula's palms broke out in a cold sweat as she snatched up her notebook and tossed it into her bag.

"Yes, of course. Where? When?" She searched the room for her shoes. Where had she kicked them?

"We can't be seen together," the caller murmured. "I don't want to end up like Jason Taylor. I can come after work. Meet me at Garcia Park in an hour."

Ursula dropped to her knees to look under the bed. "But—" The line went dead. She pulled her shoes into the open and plopped onto her butt. Damn, this thing was coming together. She resisted the urge to fist pump the air.

She jogged in Garcia Park sometimes. It wasn't the nicest

park in the area, but it wasn't far from her hotel. She could easily get there in less than an hour. But she'd promised to meet Willa. She hit the redial on her phone again. This time, the call went to voice mail.

Ursula waited for the beep and then left her message. "Willa, I got a lead. I'm meeting a witness at Garcia Park in an hour. She knows something about Aaron Michaels, and it might be exactly what we're looking for. I'll come over afterward, as soon as I'm finished. Thanks."

She took a quick shower, slapped on a bit of makeup and clean clothes. She grabbed the old umbrella standing by the door and fought to open it. Several of its ribs were broken into sharp pieces, but the fabric was waterproof and basically intact. She slipped into her coat, tossed her bag over her shoulder, the umbrella in one hand and keys to the rental car in the other, and headed out.

The moonless night air was still cold, but not as cold as last night when Jason Taylor died. Wind buffeted the umbrella and lifted it away from her face. Icy rain pelted her skin. Ice had already glazed the parking lot. She slipped twice before she reached the sedan and grabbed onto the door handle to steady herself. She fought to close the umbrella and slid behind the wheel, cold and shivering.

Slippery pavement slowed her progress, but she barely noticed the drive, because she was so focused on the meeting. What could this woman have on Aaron Michaels? She had to be another of his victims, didn't she? A live victim, willing to testify. That was more than enough to get this story into every news outlet in the country.

Aaron Michaels didn't belong on the bench. Ursula planned to prove it.

Briefly, she considered calling Detective Mason, but she dismissed the idea out of hand. The young woman was already spooked. Showing up with a cop in tow would send her running in the opposite direction.

No, Ursula had known the risks when she took on this quest. She wouldn't back down now. She was so close. By habit, she reached into her purse and groped around until she found her Taser and slipped it into her coat pocket. She never walked around alone at night without it.

When she pulled up to Garcia Park, her every nerve lit in anticipation, but the place was deserted. Foul weather had chased even the usual joggers away for the night. But the gate was unchained, wide open.

She maneuvered the rented sedan down the winding driveway, slowly, keeping the wheels on the pavement only by sheer will and tension.

Once she reached the parking lot that sat directly in front of the central pond, she pulled into an empty spot. She turned off the ignition but left her lights on. The cold and lonely park felt more than a little creepy. She shuddered.

A few minutes later, one hour from her phone call on the dot, another vehicle pulled in and parked in the spot next to hers.

A young woman was in the driver's seat, the only occupant of the non-descript vehicle. Ursula blew out a sigh of relief.

She hadn't been expecting a white van with three goons in it, but who knew?

Her heart rate slowed to something closer to normal as the young woman, dressed in a brown and yellow uniform from a local eatery, stepped out of the SUV and slipped into a hooded yellow raincoat. The poncho had the same local eatery's logo on the front.

They met on the sidewalk. Ursula held the decrepit umbrella in her left hand and stuck out her right. "Thank you for meeting with me. I'm Ursula Westfield."

The woman smelled like fried fish. She tucked a lock of mousy brown hair behind one ear and stuffed both hands in her pockets. "Yeah, well, when I heard what happened to Jason Taylor, I felt like I had no choice. I'm Stacy Albrecht. I used to be Judge Michaels' law clerk." Her pale face shone in the moonlight, and her eyes were full of tears. "Do you mind if we walk and talk? I'm so cold I can't seem to stop my legs from shaking. It warms me up to move."

She walked along the sidewalk that circled the pond, a popular track for joggers, rollerbladers and the like during better weather. Ursula matched her pace, noticing for the first time that the other woman was holding a large envelope.

Maybe she'd brought actual proof. Photos of her abuse. Ursula gently attempted to guide the conversation. "You said you wanted to talk to me about Michaels?"

Stacy nodded. "He has affairs with his law clerks. He's having an affair now with Tiffany Strong."

"I met her earlier today. Intense young woman." Ursula tugged her coat more tightly around her body. Her fingers were cold claws on the grip of the umbrella's handle. "But you said you didn't want to end up like Jason Taylor. Was there some connection between Michaels and Taylor?"

"That's not the problem. It's Tiffany's failure." The younger woman slowed and turned to face Ursula, her thin lips twisting as she frowned. "She's not strong enough. She could never protect Aaron. See, that's why I had to do it, Miss Westfield. Because Tiffany's too weak."

Quickly, smoothly, Stacy's hand slid out of her pocket.

Stacy lunged at her, right arm extended, holding a blade that glinted in the weak lamplight.

Ursula jerked back in stunned surprise. Too late.

She pin-wheeled backward, fear coalescing in her stomach like spoiled milk. She dropped the umbrella, and it collapsed. Sleet pelted her body. Her teeth chattered.

Stacy lunged forward again, slicing the knife through the air.

Ursula spun left. Her heel caught on a rock, sending her stumbling backward. She tripped on the umbrella and fell onto her back in the muddy grass. A hot stinging pain erupted in her side, and she realized through building terror that she'd been cut. She scrambled to push herself to her feet.

"That stupid fool. She thinks he loves her, but she has no idea what it takes to keep a man like Aaron." Stacy's words were shrill now. The look in her eyes was almost maniacal, as she continued to stalk Ursula, lunging and slicing with the bloody blade.

Ursula backed up, keeping her eyes on Stacy, looking for an opening. Any opening.

God, why hadn't she called Mason?

She cupped a hand to her aching side and winced as the sticky heat of her blood coated her fingers.

"You don't have to do this, Stacy." Ursula held up her free left hand defensively as she continued to walk backward, off the side of the sidewalk and onto the grass. "He's not worthy of you. He's not who you think he is."

"Shut up. You shut up about him." Stacy brandished the dagger threateningly and kept coming, her motions growing more agitated by the second. "He made a terrible mistake, choosing her over me. He'll realize that now. Jason is dead. You'll be dead. No one will know."

Ursula swallowed hard and strained to see the grass in her peripheral vision as she spoke in a calm voice. "You're probably right. She thinks she's younger and prettier than you, but she doesn't understand what you're willing to do for him."

Stacy nodded breathlessly. "Exactly."

Without taking a moment's rest, Stacy barreled at Ursula like a bull charges the red cape, throwing all of her body weight and momentum behind a final swift and lethal strike.

Ursula's Taser was in her right coat pocket. But her right hand covered the gash in her side, so she couldn't wrestle the Taser out in time.

She dropped low and, quick as a snake strike, snatched up the umbrella. She brandished it in front of her body to deflect Stacy's slashing blow.

The umbrella was a Hail Mary. But it was all she had. And it did nothing to slow Stacy's determination. Or her momentum.

Ursula squeezed her eyes closed with a silent prayer as Stacy's body connected with hers, the useless umbrella between them.

They toppled to the ground with a bone-jarring crash.

Ursula screamed in agony.

Her stomach and chest felt hot. So hot. Sticky blood pooled over her. The pain in her torso was excruciating. She couldn't bear it.

Stacy's full weight held Ursula to the ground as her vision went black.

CHAPTER EIGHT

"YOU'RE LUCKY TO BE alive," Willa said from the doorway of Ursula's hospital room the next day.

Ursula looked up from the plastic container of pudding she'd been eating and managed a weak smile. "That's the understatement of the year."

Willa walked closer to her hospital bed. She rested a hand on her shoulder. "How's your head feeling now?"

The doctors said she'd been knocked unconscious when Stacy tackled her and her head hit a rock. "Like a Japanese drummer is playing *Wipeout* on my brain." She grinned and squeezed Willa's hand. "My stomach doesn't feel all that great, either."

Stacy had lacerated her side, just under her ribcage. But the strike had missed all vital organs. The cut required stitches, but she'd survived.

"You were a lot luckier than Jason Taylor," Willa said, softly.

"Yes." Ursula shuddered when she thought about how close she'd come to joining Jason in death. "Thanks for coming to pick me up. They're finishing my discharge papers now."

But Willa wasn't about to let her off the hook so easily. "That was a reckless thing you did, going out there alone. What the hell were you thinking?"

"I know, I know. And you have every right to rip into me, but can you just give me a day or two? I'm worn out."

Willa's gaze softened a little, and she shook her head. But she didn't reply. Instead, she pulled a bouquet of flowers from behind her back with a flourish.

"Gerbera daisies are my favorite," Ursula said, tears leaking from her eyes. She felt weak after the attack. It seemed she cried at the least little things. She cleared her throat. "How is Stacy Albrecht?"

"Detective Mason said she's touch and go." Willa shook her head again. "When she charged at you that last time, she landed on that old umbrella at an odd angle, and somehow one of the broken ribs on it punctured her chest and nicked her heart."

Ursula gasped. She'd been fighting for her life, but she hadn't intended to kill Stacy in the process.

"She'll survive." Willa's sympathy didn't extend as far as Ursula's. "But she killed a man in his prime and tried to murder you. She'll be prosecuted."

"But that look in her eyes, Willa. She's mentally ill. Her relationship with Michaels pushed her over the edge." Ursula shuddered.

"If that's true, her lawyer will present those defenses to the court." Willa frowned. "The justice system has a way of sorting these things out. You do your job, and we'll do ours."

Ursula didn't have the energy to argue. She lay back against the pillow and closed her eyes a minute.

"I have some good news, too. I never got a chance to tell you what I learned about Judge Michaels." Willa reached under her arm, grabbed a newspaper and tossed it onto the hospital bed.

Puzzled, Ursula picked up the newspaper and gasped when she saw Judge Aaron Michaels staring back at her in black and white. She read the first paragraph aloud.

"Circuit Court Judge Aaron Michaels was arrested on charges of multiple counts of corruption. Michaels is accused of accepting kickbacks from two private juvenile detention centers. It is alleged that Michaels received the money in exchange for sending youths to the private detention centers instead of sentencing them to community service or probation. Judge Michaels was recently accused of sexual harassment of his law clerks, including a decades-old rape accusation that hit airwaves yesterday in the wake of his wife's petition for divorce."

Ursula sat back, stunned. "Holy cow. Kids for cash? How did this come out?"

"Turns out that after Stacy attacked you, Detective Mason persuaded Tiffany Strong to come clean. The pictures of Millie Taylor were found in her son's briefcase. And Michaels' wife had been having him followed. She wanted a divorce. She handed over an entire box of evidence to Detective Mason before she walked out." Willa shrugged. "I'd heard rumors about the kickbacks investigation a while ago."

Ursula looked at her. "Will he be convicted?"

"Not for what he did to Millie Taylor." Willa shook her head. "But the corruption has been going on for years. One boy, sent away at the age of twelve, was killed at fourteen by another boy. Michaels will go to prison for a long time."

Ursula looked down at her hands and nodded.

Willa sat on the chair next to the bed and folded her hands across her knee. "I know how much you wanted justice for Millie Taylor. And for her son. But Michaels didn't kill Millie, and the rape case is simply too old to prove. And he didn't kill Jason Taylor. Stacy did that on her own."

"I understand. He's going to prison. I guess I'll have to be satisfied with that," Ursula took a deep breath and looked up again. "Unless I can find a way to tie him to those murders someday."

Willa stood and smiled expectantly. "George canceled your hotel room and insisted you stay with us. He swears he'll keep the dogs from jumping on you. Let's get the hell out of here."

Ursula gazed down at the newspaper in her lap and bittersweet tears blurred her vision. She could never give Millie or Jason back what they'd lost, but Judge Aaron Michaels' life was in shambles. His career was over, his family had abandoned him and he would be in prison for a long time.

It would have to be enough.

Goodbye, Millie. I wish I'd had the chance to know you.

Ursula set the newspaper aside and swung her legs off the bed.

"Let's go."

THE END

FAIR
JUSTICE

*Thank you to some of the best readers in the world:
Beth Nagorsky (Desiree Rothchild) and John Kuvacas
(Antoine Crowe) for participating in our character naming
giveaways which make this book a bit more personal and
fun for all of us.*

And for Wilhelmina Boersma, trailblazer extraordinaire.

CAST OF PRIMARY CHARACTERS

Judge Wilhelmina Carson
George Carson

Mike Caldwell
Lydia Gregg
Roger Madsen
Annalisa Fantz
Dale Fantz
Bradley Fletcher
Walter Danbury
Chuck Bartow
Cathy Bartow

CHAPTER ONE

MIKE CALDWELL STARED AT the jewel-colored bottles lined up behind the Sunset Bar at George's Place and briefly wished he'd come an hour early to knock back a few before his date arrived…even though she was the same date he'd been lucky enough to have for the better part of a decade.

Sweet Lydia.

He almost never felt awkward or nervous around her. Except when he knew something he'd planned to say would piss her off, or, apparently, when he knew he was about to propose.

And he would do both tonight before he left town.

He winced and waved the bartender over. "Let me have your best whiskey, neat."

His boss, News Director Roger Madsen, threw a major wrench in his plans an hour ago. An assignment too good to turn down. A story that would make his career, if he handled it right. A married man needed a good job. Lydia would see that.

"Caldwell, this thing may turn out to be a bust," Madsen had said when he called Mike into the office to give him the assignment. "But after that water catastrophe in Flint, Michigan, and environmentalism run amok in the country…well, we can't afford to ignore a potential story like criminal polluting."

Mike's heart skipped a beat. It was the first time Madsen had given him any assignment, let alone one that could have national news potential. "What's the claim?"

"Fletcher Textiles, a carpet manufacturer up in Peru, Florida. Not far from the Georgia state line. A local woman says they're dumping toxic waste into the drinking water. She says one of the workers found solid proof, and now he's disappeared. She's worried about him. Not exactly a whistleblower, but close enough to take a look." Madsen held an unlit cigar between his fingers as if he could still smoke in the office like news directors of old. "Frankly, if I was sure it was a story, I'd send someone with more experience. But if I was sure it wasn't a story, we wouldn't go at all. Everybody else is covering the hurricane down in the Caribbean, and you're always bugging me for an opportunity. So it's yours."

"I understand," Mike said, nodding like the eager young reporter he surely was. "When would I need to go?"

"Tomorrow. Stay a few days. Dig around. See whether there's anything worth investigating or not. Keep me posted." Madsen waved him out the door as he reached for his clamoring phone. "Everything we know so far was sent to your email inbox."

It wasn't until Mike's excitement slowed that he realized what he'd done. Lydia was going to kill him.

The bartender slid a crystal glass across the bar, and Mike glanced at his watch before powering down the amber liquid in one swallow. It burned a welcome path of warmth straight to his stomach. Liquid courage.

Everything would be fine. He'd explain to Lydia, and she'd be angry, but she'd get over it. Eventually. Maybe.

Judge Willa Carson walked into the Sunset Bar still wearing her business suit. She walked around like her husband owned the place. She came over and sat beside him. "Sapphire and tonic, and whatever my friend is drinking," she said to the bartender before clapping a hand on Mike's shoulder and giving him a friendly squeeze. "So tonight's the big night? George has the pastry chef doing something amazing. Hand it over."

She held out a palm and Mike couldn't help but be swept up by her enthusiasm. He reached into his pocket and fished around, producing a gleaming black box. He handed it to her.

Willa cracked the box open and let out a gasp that settled Mike's nerves some.

"It's quite literally perfect, Mike," Willa said, her eyes going suspiciously glassy.

The praise meant a lot coming from the notoriously tough federal judge, and his nerves settled a little more.

"Thanks." Mike gave a halting nod and Willa's brow furrowed.

"You don't honestly think there's a chance she'll say no, do you?"

"I think there's a chance she'll say yes and then take it back once I give her the news," he admitted ruefully.

"What news?" Willa closed the ring box and placed it on the bar.

"That I can't go with her to Alabama for the week. Her parents' fiftieth wedding anniversary. They have a huge family thing planned. Been working on it for months." He shrugged helplessly. "But opportunity came knocking, and I had to answer the door."

Willa's eyes narrowed. "What kind of opportunity?"

"A toxic waste story up in Peru, Florida. The kind of

irresponsible corporate behavior that ruins communities and gets CEOs indicted." Mike could hear the excitement in his own voice. He'd need to tone that down when he told Lydia. But dammit, this was big. Or it could be. He had a right to be excited.

"In other words, the kind of story that gives a young network reporter like you a chance to climb the ladder from live shots behind the camera to features." Willa took another sip and shook her head.

"Exactly."

"More likely to be a wild goose chase. CEOs are savvy enough not to get involved in shady practices that have potential criminal penalties attached. We levy big fines and put CEOs in jail these days." Willa frowned and placed a hand on his arm.

"I know but—"

"Criminals are dangerous, Mike. You spent enough time in my courtroom to learn that much, didn't you?" She patted her pockets as if searching for something.

"All I'm supposed to do is ask around. How dangerous can that be?" He'd never have had the nerve to argue with her in public, but it was just the two of them here.

"Don't mess this up." Willa shook her head as she pulled a Partagas cigar from her jacket. "There will always be tension between your job and your family if you're halfway good at either. Lydia's a special woman. You won't find anyone who loves you more."

"Believe me, I know," he nodded, miserably. "But chances like this won't come my way every day, either. It's been two years since I stopped covering cops and courts here, Judge Carson. I'm ready for a bigger job, and this story can push me right into Eyes on Eight if I play it right."

The bartender brought their drinks and Willa raised her glass in a toast. Mike raised his, too, and clinked the glasses before they sipped. The whiskey was starting to loosen him up.

"What's the name of the business?" Willa's tone took on the demanding quality he'd seen her use on the bench.

"Fletcher Textiles. A whistleblower is missing. Guy named Chuck Bartow. People in the town are sick. Sounds like a textbook case of toxic waste dumping, doesn't it?" Mike asked.

Willa nodded. "Which is why you have to figure it's not."

He raised his eyebrows but didn't reply.

"I'll ask around. I've got colleagues in that area. If there's anything going on, they'll know about it." She took another sip of her gin.

Before Mike could ask her not to interfere, George came breezing through the double kitchen doors, the leather soles of his cap-toed brogue dress shoes clicking on the marble floor.

"Mike!" He closed the distance between them and shook Mike's hand before slipping an affectionate arm around his wife's waist. "Let's have a look."

Willa held up the open ring box, and George let out a low whistle. "Beautiful. She'll love it."

Mike frowned again, "I hope so."

George cast a questioning glance toward Willa.

Before he could say more, the restaurant door swung open, and Lydia walked in, with a quick wave, she swept past Desiree at the hostess station. Her cheeks were pink from the cold, but her beaming smile warmed Mike to the core.

George slid the ring box into his pocket.

After small talk, and a warning scowl from Willa for Mike's eyes only, George led them to their table for two with a view of Hillsborough Bay. Once they were seated, George excused himself to tend to other guests, leaving Mike and Lydia alone.

Mike almost wished he could call George back. He could use the buffer. *Coward.*

He asked, "How were things at the hospital today?" Lydia worked as a nurse at Tampa Southern, the only level-one trauma center in the Bay area. More than once, she'd helped him with access to victims in cases he'd reported. They made a good team, personally and professionally.

"Like every day. Crazy busy." Lydia slipped her coat off. She'd donned his favorite red dress with the sweetheart neckline that made her look like a million bucks. "I swear, it's the full moon or something driving people to do stupid stuff that gets them injured, you know?"

She opened the elegant leather menu and began scanning it quickly. "I'm starved. I skipped lunch because I love the food here."

Mike opened his menu, but he wasn't hungry. He'd planned to tell her about the assignment after he proposed, hoping her excitement over the engagement would soften her anger. Now, though, going through the whole dinner with bad news hanging over him seemed intolerable. He closed the menu with a snap.

"Look," he said in a rush, "I have to tell you something, and you're not going to be happy."

Her head shot up, and her smile slid away. She cocked her head and waited.

The waiter came at that moment, bearing two glasses of red wine and an appetizer.

"Did you order ahead?" she asked, surprise taking the edge off her expected irritation. She eyed the fancy charcuterie board and all the selections, a grin tugging at the corners of her mouth once again. "Brie and figs...and is that Stilton? You know me so well."

She snatched up a fancy cracker and slathered it with soft, creamy cheese before setting a fig on top.

"When I put this in my mouth, you start talking. It will be like anesthesia for your bad news. Ready?" She popped the cracker in her mouth and groaned in pleasure as she chewed.

He launched in with no further hesitation. "Our best investigative reporter has the flu, and everybody else is covering the hurricane, so the boss offered me an Eyes on Eight slot for next week." He cleared his throat. "I have to leave tomorrow morning."

He broke off as her eyes closed and her body caved in on itself like she'd been sucker punched. He gave her a second to swallow her food before continuing softly. "I'd be gone for about three days, that's all. I can meet you in Fair Hope as soon as I'm done. I'm so sorry, Lyd—"

"I know how important your career is, Mike," she cut in, holding a palm out, fire flashing in her eyes. "I know how cut-throat it is, and how hard you work. But it's my parents' *fiftieth*. You promised me you wouldn't bail on us."

He'd expected her to be pissed off and now he almost wished for it. Because instead, she looked heartsick, which he simply couldn't take.

Antoine, their waiter, passed by and Mike stopped him with a hand. "Can you thank George for selecting such a lovely bottle of wine for us?"

It was the pre-arranged signal sending Antoine into the kitchen to return with the ring. Only that wasn't supposed to happen until dessert. Antoine eyed Mike in confusion. "Uh, yes, yes of course."

"Thank you," Mike added with an encouraging smile.

Antoine rushed off, and Mike turned his attention back to Lydia. He'd planned a thousand ways to say the words, but the right moment was now. He took a gulp from his water glass and leaned in to take her hand.

"You don't want me to go? I don't go. Because this?" he gave her hand a squeeze. "Us? Matters to me more than anything else. We're both driven, and we both want to succeed. I wouldn't change that. But I will choose you every time, Lydia. You have to know that."

Antoine approached and hovered in the background. Mike waved him in. He set a gorgeous antique Herend plate in front of Lydia with a chocolate orb in the center, surrounded by raspberries and topped with a nest of golden, spun sugar. Nestled inside the chocolate was the engagement ring, kissed by the candlelight, a sparkling light show.

Mike stood and rounded the table to kneel before Lydia. Her face was white with shock and tears swam in her eyes.

"You are everything to me, Lydia, and I want to spend the rest of my life with you." He plucked the diamond from its nest and held it out, heart hammering. "Will you marry me?"

When her face crumpled and she began to sob, his hands went ice cold. What if she said no?

"We've been together five years, Mike." She sniffled on a half-hysterical laugh, sticking out a trembling left hand. "I thought you'd never ask."

He slid the ring on her finger, rocked with relief and joy.

"Oh my," she said, staring down at her hand. "It's beautiful."

The room had gone silent around them, and Mike shot a glance over his shoulder to see Willa and George looking on from afar. He gave them a thumb's up and grinned.

"She said yes," he called.

The restaurant exploded with applause as Lydia held up her hand for all to see.

Mike rose to his feet and pressed a kiss to her lips. He'd landed the best girl in Tampa, and she'd already forgiven him. Over Lydia's shoulder, he caught a glimpse of Willa's troubled frown and his euphoria evaporated just as quickly as it had arrived.

Now, if only his luck would hold and he could get this story right. He'd need photographs, interviews. Fletcher Textiles was hurting the people of Peru, and he would prove it. He'd get the Eyes on Eight gig and everything would be perfect.

CHAPTER TWO

"YOU HAVE ARRIVED AT your destination," the cool, female voice announced from his phone as he glanced down to see the blinking house icon beside the address he'd entered into the GPS.

Mike looked out his window to find a tall but narrow brick building to his right. Once a private home, it was now a bed and breakfast. On the patchy lawn, nestled between tiny bushels of pink blossoms, sat a sign that read "The Fantz House." He turned off his engine.

Inside, Annalisa Fantz would be waiting for him, ready to tell her story. He squared his shoulders, more than prepared to listen.

He'd spent most of his tenure at the television station in the background, behind the lens, but he knew this first interview could go a lot of ways. Some people were frank, matter-of-fact. Others were weepy. Some were spitting with rage.

But there was only one way to find out which type of person Annalisa Franz would be.

Plucking his video camera and microphone from the trunk,

he marched up the flagstones across the wide, wrap-around porch, glancing only momentarily at the cheery little "Welcome" sign on the door before ringing the bell.

In less than an instant, the door swung open.

"How can I help you?" The woman was frail and thin, so pale that she was nearly translucent except for the angry purple bags beneath dark, sunken eyes. Gray hair peeked out in wisps from beneath the floral scarf wrapped around her head. She wiped bony hands on a stained white apron.

"Mike Caldwell. From EBC—"

She nodded before he could finish. "Yes, yes, of course. I start cooking, and the whole world just flies out of my head. Come in, come in."

She led him through the narrow halls toward the very back of the house and into a small, tidy kitchen. The appliances were old—cheap white models from decades before, chipped but clean. Just in front of the windows sat a tiny white table and chairs. After a moment, Mike noticed that they were not alone.

Perched in front of the table was a child. He was sitting in a wheelchair that was nearly as old as everything else in the kitchen and, without a doubt, much older than the boy.

"Hello, nice to meet you. I'm Mike Caldwell." Mike extended his hand.

The boy took it, offering a weak smile.

"Dale, introduce yourself," Annalisa murmured and stood behind the cutting board full of half-chopped root vegetables. He glanced at her for a moment before turning his attention back to Mike.

"I'm sorry, Mr. Caldwell. I'm Dale Fantz." His voice was wheezy. "It's a pleasure to meet you."

"My son." Annalisa nodded, picked up her knife, and resumed chopping.

But Mike had figured that much out for himself. Dale was the reason for this interview.

From the files his boss had forwarded, he knew only a few details. Dale was thirteen, but he seemed much smaller than a boy his age should be. About four years ago, he had developed an illness that had ravaged his body and still couldn't be explained. Mrs. Fantz blamed the textile plant's new carpet mill. A few months after production started, she claimed more kids were absent from school and flocking to doctors than the town had ever seen before.

Like his mother, Dale was pale and thin, but the vitality that exuded from Annalisa, hard-boned as she was, was absent from her son. He sat hunched over, his clothes much too big for him, a husk of a person. If Mike allowed the silence to continue, he would be able to count the boy's breaths from his rattling inhales and whistling exhales.

Mike's chest ached in sympathy, and it was an effort not to chatter just to fill the room with another, less heart-wrenching sound.

The doorbell rang. Annalisa looked at her son. "Dale, would you mind answering the door and then going to your room and finish your homework?"

The boy wheeled himself from the room without a word of protest, and Annalisa let out a little sigh.

"He's never going to do that homework unless I stand over him and watch him do it, you know. That'll be Cathy Bartow at the door. It's her husband, Chuck, who's missing." She offered Mike a small smile, then something clicked behind her eyes, and she said. "Oh, goodness, how rude I've been.

You must be thirsty after your long trip. What can I get for you?"

"Water is fine," Mike said.

Annalisa pursed her lips for a moment and then nodded. From the fridge, she pulled a two-gallon water tub and filled three glasses before setting one in front of Mike.

"Oh, you didn't have to do that. Tap water is—" He heard Dale's quiet murmur and a woman's louder voice in the foyer. The boy's wheelchair rolled down the hallway, and soft footsteps came toward the kitchen.

"It'd be better not to drink the water while you're here." Annalisa nodded at the glass as she shoved her hands into her apron pockets.

"Something wrong with your water?"

A young woman walked into the room just as Mike asked the question. "Docs say no way of knowing what caused Dale's condition. Could be the soil. The food. The milk. Better safe than sorry, though. That's for sure."

Annalisa shrugged. "Mr. Caldwell, this is Cathy Bartow."

The younger woman was dressed in jeans and a sweatshirt, sneakers on her feet. Her hair was gathered into a messy knot at the base of her neck. She shook his hand briefly and turned to her friend. "I can't stay, Annalisa. I've got to pick up Charlie at my mom's. I would have called to let you know, but something has happened to my damn cell phone..."

"Maybe I can come by and talk to you tomorrow, Mrs. Bartow?" Mike asked.

She nodded absently.

He gave her his business card.

She stuffed it into her pocket without reading it. "I'll call you, Annalisa," she said on her way out.

Annalisa clucked her tongue as Cathy dashed from the room. "She's beside herself. Chuck isn't the kind of guy to just go on a lark without telling his family."

"Anybody call the police? Make a report?" In Tampa, calling the police would have been the very first thing a wife would have done.

Annalisa shrugged again and sipped from one of the water glasses. "You'll need to ask Cathy. I'm not sure what she's done. I just know something's not right at that factory. We've all begged Chuck to stop sticking his nose into places where it doesn't belong…"

He wasn't going to get any more answers on that score, so he tried a new approach. "Mrs. Fantz, how long have you lived here?"

"In this house, a little better than a year." She returned to her chopping.

"Where'd you live before? When Dale first got sick?"

"Over in Peru. About seven years ago, right after my husband passed, I moved from Texas into my mother's boarding house over there. Made sense. I was alone with Dale. We could help each other out." She'd returned to her chopping, punctuating her words with the knife blade against the board. "Back then, of course, mother's place was mostly for migrant farm workers. Short-term. So that families had a cozy place to stay before they moved on to the next crop in season somewhere else, you know?"

"We have migrant workers like that in the Tampa area, too." Mike nodded again.

"Before the factory expanded, the town was pretty much split in two groups, farmers and textile workers. Since the expansion, not many farms anymore." She chopped the veggies in a mesmerizing rhythm as the big knife blade whacked the cutting board. "Not a whole lot of towns around like Peru, but we felt lucky to have the factory. It brought jobs and a bit of security to all of us back then."

Mike had driven through lots of farmland on the way up here "So what happened to the farmland over in Peru? The factory bought up the acreage for the expansion?"

Annalisa paused in her chopping and leaned back on her worn laminated counter. She shrugged again. "About a year after the factory began producing the new carpet, the crops were gone. No more farm workers."

"What do you mean?" Mike felt a twinge in his gut and pushed the water glass aside.

"Nothing grew." She frowned and shook her head. "I remember going to the town council, right back when Dale started with his cough, and city council would say the craziest things just to get people to stop suggesting that the factory had anything to do with what was happening with the crops, with Dale and the others. Well, of course, I knew better." She clicked her tongue.

His mouth dried up. He sipped the water, but it didn't help. "And what exactly *was* happening with Dale?"

"Well, at first the docs thought he had meningitis. But by the third trip to the hospital, they said no." Annalisa shook her head. "Never figured it out, really. His organs were just shutting down. And he wasn't the only one. A few kids were worse off, but their parents… Let's just say we all learned real quick not to go poking around."

Mike felt the small hairs rise on his neck and gooseflesh on his arms. *Good grief, man. Get a grip.* "What happened when you questioned the situation at the town counsel?"

"I went back to one of those council meetings. Spoke my piece. Even tried to get a reporter from Jacksonville involved." She shook her head and looked at the floor. "Then it was months of odd little problems with my electric, my water, anything you can name. And the bank called in my mortgage on the boarding house out of the blue. I couldn't pay it."

Mike frowned. "So that's when you moved here?"

"We didn't want to leave our friends. Peru's only five miles away and this is about twice the mortgage of the old place, but..." She met his gaze. "When your child's life is on the line, there's nothing you can do, you know?"

"And has Dale's health improved? Since the move, I mean?" He heard the hope in his voice.

Annalisa's face somehow managed to blanch from pale to ghostly. "Docs say the decline has slowed."

She meant the damage was already done. "Honestly, Mrs. Fantz, I'm not sure we've got much to go on here. I'll do what I can. Ask around—"

Annalisa held up her hand. "I don't mean to be rude, Mr. Caldwell, but you might want to consider keeping your reasons for visiting Peru to yourself."

Mike opened his mouth to speak, but she shushed him with a wave.

"You don't know what it's like. What they can do. Just be safe. Think about Chuck Bartow gone missing and don't tell a soul why you're here."

He frowned at the warning in her voice and wondered how she expected him to dig up anything incriminating without asking the right people the right questions. "I'll keep that in mind."

They talked a little more, and she fed him a surprisingly good home-cooked meal, and he left for his hotel.

He wrote up his notes from the interview and emailed them to his boss. He said it seemed like further investigation of her claims was warranted. There was something going on here, and the coincidental timing didn't pass the smell test.

He hadn't learned anything about the missing man, so his email emphasized the dying crops and the sick kids. The environmental story could be newsworthy, assuming he could find any real evidence. Either the regulations were inadequate to protect the people of Peru, or the regulations existed and were violated. Similar environmental tragedies had been surfacing around the country in recent years. Peru could be another one, he told Madsen.

Mrs. Fantz said there had been no reports about any of these troubles on local or national media, which should make the story more enticing to his boss. He promised to send video and still shots tomorrow.

Mike was feeling pretty good, though, because he hadn't spoiled Lydia's plans unnecessarily. Something was going on here in Peru. But what?

CHAPTER THREE

BEFORE THE SUN PEEKED over the horizon the next morning, Mike was already climbing into his car, ready to document whatever he found when he drove into the town of Peru. He needed enough of something, anything, to make further investigation worthwhile. Madsen had made that much perfectly clear.

Peru was the kind of town where strangers would be noticed. But today was Sunday, and the Fletcher Textiles factory was closed. It was a good time to check out the area. He'd shoot his raw video without interruptions or interfering with operations. The factory was on private property, so he'd need permission to go inside, anyway. Which meant he'd come back tomorrow to finish up.

The drive into Peru wound through what had been farmland for generations. The fields lay fallow, just as Annalisa Fantz said. Even a mile away, as he passed the "Welcome to Peru, where everyone is family" sign, a faint smell permeated the air and grew stronger as he approached Fletcher Textiles. A stringent, chemical smell, and something caustic and sour that stuck in the back of his throat. He opened his mouth to breathe. Better to taste the noxious fumes than to feel them burn inside his nostrils.

Grass and weeds along the shoulders of the road and in the ditches were dead brown and disappeared altogether as the factory came into view. Bare trees made the scene foreboding.

He wasn't a gardener. Most of the houseplants he'd tried to grow over the years died away. Dead plants alone didn't necessarily mean illegal polluting was the cause. Could be a bunch of lousy farmers, like him.

"Objectivity is key," he mumbled Madsen's mantra under his breath, pushing away the nagging memory of Annalisa Fantz's voice and Dale Fantz in his old wheelchair. Mike turned onto the cross street in front of the factory.

As he'd expected, the area was vacant at this hour, every window of the brick building darkened. He parked, stepped out of the car, and made his way over. He looked around before ducking under the mechanical armed security gate to traipse up the winding driveway to the factory itself. He was trespassing, but he didn't intend to harm anything. He just wanted to see the place. Get a feel for it.

He pulled his phone from his pocket. As he moved, he used his camera phone, careful of his angles and settings to get the clearest shots. None of these photos could be published without permission, but if Fletcher Textiles had nothing to hide, their permission should be easy enough to get later. Besides, he worked in TV. Still photos would be of limited use on the air. When he got permission, he'd come back for video.

He moved into the rising sun, juxtaposing a rolling green hill behind the factory against the barren land in front of it for context.

From the outside, Fletcher Textiles was a factory like any other, complete with smoke stacks and an employee-only patio. But there was no way of photographing the eerie calm that enclosed the place like a bubble. The total, unnerving silence. Sure, it was Sunday and the place was closed and lacked whooshing cars and chattering people, but the silence was unnerving for a different reason, one he couldn't quite pinpoint.

He followed the walking trail on the grounds until he reached a small pond and the wood beyond on the edge of the property. Leaves rustled at his feet, and he stopped short, struck suddenly by what was missing.

No chirping. The first rays of sun were blazing paths of light through the trees, but there were no birds to greet the new day. No gentle hum of crickets or buzz of insects. No mosquitos, even.

He glanced at the line of trees, then picked up a rock and threw it into the mass of leaves.

Nothing moved.

Nothing skittered or croaked or rustled.

Just a crunch of leaves and then the dense, complete silence resumed. As if there were no living creatures anywhere.

Bending low and contorting his body, Mike photographed it all. The pond, which was covered by a weird shimmering film, the strange pockets of mud on the ground, everything he could shoot. The sun was already higher in the sky than he'd planned by the time he finished.

Soon, people would be heading to church and opening their businesses, and he wanted to be back in his hotel room when they did, carefully studying his photos so he could figure out his next step. And he wanted to interview Cathy Bartow today, too.

When he reached the wrought iron gates again, he glanced

around one last time before ducking below the security postern and walking toward his car.

From behind him, a chipper male voice called out, and Mike turned, careful to look just as friendly as the voice sounded as he dropped his phone into his oversized jacket pocket.

"Hey buddy, you lost? Can I help you with something?" The man walking toward him was built like a snowman with a mustache. His tiny head sat perched on his rounded body without a neck to speak of, and when he waved a chubby hand, Mike was left with no option but to stop and reply.

"Oh, no, I'm sorry. Visiting town and out for a hike." Mike pointed to his hiking boots as proof.

"Ah, well. I was thinking you might've come by looking for work," the man said.

Mike considered for a moment, weighing his options, but then he heard Annalisa's voice in his head again, and he couldn't ignore her warning to keep the reasons for his interest in the factory to himself. "Are they hiring?"

"Just so happens, we are." He stuck his hand out to Mike. "Bradley Fletcher, CEO of Fletcher Textiles."

"Wow, quite the honor." Mike took his hand, pumping it twice before releasing him.

Fletcher chuckled. "Now, you're a flatterer."

"What brings the CEO here on a Sunday morning?" Mike asked, trying to keep his tone light.

"I imagine most men with two-year-old twin boys would find themselves running to work whenever they can." Fletcher chuckled again. "Easier job by far."

"Oh," Mike nodded, then, more carefully, "Do you and your family live here in Peru?"

Fletcher's eyebrows shot up a fraction, but his easy smile

returned in a quick moment. "Unfortunately, no. Easier for the wife to have a short commute to her office. Besides, I'm sure my employees are happier not running into the boss on their personal time."

Mike forced a smile. "I'm sure."

Fletcher shrugged. "Would you like a tour of the place? I have a bit of time before I need to get to work."

Mike shook his head. "I'd better get going."

Fletcher shoved his hands in his pockets and nodded. "And hey, the offer stands. If you're interested in a job, be sure to stop back during business hours, okay?"

His jolly demeanor never faltered, but Mike felt he'd chosen his words carefully throughout the conversation.

Business hours. Got it.

Mike nodded and smiled and then jogged back to his car. Had Fletcher seen him taking pictures? Not likely. If he'd seen, he'd have said something, right?

Bradley Fletcher was probably just like every other person on earth. He didn't care about a damn thing unless he knew for a fact it directly affected him. Fletcher was probably there doing exactly what he'd said. Taking a break from his twin toddlers for a few hours.

Mike hurried back to his hotel. So far, he had nothing solid to support a story. Nothing but creepy feelings and guesses. He needed to find proof before Madsen would okay the project. But what?

After uploading the pictures to his laptop, he scrolled through each one, careful to take note of the strange coating on the surface of the pond when the light hit it the right way, the way even the dirt on the ground looked discolored, unnatural.

He wrote a quick note to Madsen and selected the best of the images and pasted them into the email. He double checked the three images. A picture of the factory. A photo of the skeletal trees and bare ground. And an image of the iridescent film on the pond.

The last image was the most striking of the images, and he looked at it a little longer before scrolling over to send the email.

Which was when he saw it.

At first, he thought it was a misshapen branch, something that had fallen into the pond along with the autumn leaves.

He leaned closer, his heart pumping faster as he stretched the image to twice its size.

No tree—not even the sickly ones he'd seen all over Peru— had coloring like this one. Almost gray, and withered. And no branch had such a thick trunk with such close, tiny twigs.

Five of them.

All reaching blindly for something Mike couldn't see.

CHAPTER FOUR

MIKE DROVE ALL THE way into the city to find a printing shop. By four o'clock, he had everything he needed to visit the Peru Sheriff's office.

When he walked through the glass doors and into the little reception area, a middle-aged woman greeted him by holding up a finger and continuing her discussion with whoever was on the other end of her phone call.

"No, Mama, I know that." She let out an exasperated breath, rolling her eyes as the phone buzzed against her ear. She hung up the receiver with a bang.

"What can I do you for?" she drawled with a harried smile.

"My name is Mike Caldwell. I sent an email earlier today and—"

She held up her impatient finger again and flicked through a few papers on her desk. "So you did. It's Sunday. If you could come back tomorrow—"

"I'm sorry, ma'am, but that won't work." He shook his head. "I need to speak to the Sheriff today, while we still have daylight."

She pursed her lips, then picked up the phone again and punched in the number with practiced speed. "That reporter from Tampa, Caldwell, is here asking to see you."

A pause.

"He says it's important."

Another pause.

She slammed down the phone, pushed away from her desk, and held the door open for him. "The office that says Sheriff on the door. Go right in."

Mike ignored the snap of the door closing behind him as he walked past a couple of bored-looking deputies scribbling on paperwork.

When he reached the right office, he knocked before pushing the frosted glass open and stepping inside. An older man, looking as bored as his officers, but with that extra air of annoyance that made talking to him even less inviting, sat behind the desk. He ran a palm over his bristly salt-and-pepper goatee before gesturing to the hard seat in front of his desk.

Mike sat down. "Thanks for seeing me, Sheriff—"

"Danbury," he added gruffly. "Walter Danbury. You're Michael Caldwell. With EBC Network News, out of Tampa."

"Right."

"What was it you needed?" He glanced at the clock. "I haven't been home on time for dinner in about two weeks, and I either make it home tonight or find myself a new wife. Mind you, it wouldn't be a half-bad prospect if there was another woman on earth who could cook like she does."

Mike offered him a little smile. "In that case, I think I have bad news for you."

The Sheriff blew out a sigh and then, apparently catching his own rudeness, added, "Look, I'm sorry Mr. Caldwell, but I've had people barging through my door, banging on about that factory since the day it opened, so if you think you're going to tell me something new—"

"Let me show you." Mike reached into his bag and slid the enlarged photograph of the pond across the worn desk between them.

"What? The retention pond? It's always a little murky. Same as near any other industrial factory."

Mike pointed to the photo. "This."

Sherriff Danbury blinked down at it for a fraction of a second. "Why, that's just a branch."

"I believe that is a human hand," Mike said quietly.

Danbury looked, narrowing his eyes until he blanched. "I do see what you mean." He cleared his throat and tugged at his collar. He reached over to pick up the phone and dialed. "Before we get everybody all excited, let's go out to the site. You can show me exactly where you were standing when you shot this picture."

Mike followed the Sherriff's cruiser back to the factory, and two hours later, the eerie silence was filled with the eerier sound of a crane lifting what was left of a human body from the water.

Sheriff Danbury said he could watch, but no video or still photos on the factory property were allowed. Mike argued and lost. Officials milled around, processing the scene, conferring with each other over cooling cups of coffee as Mike looked on, shocked.

Although the corpse was in terrible condition, Chuck Bartow's nametag was still visible on his shirt. According to what Mike could hear from his spot right behind the sawhorses and crime tape, Bartow'd been a heavy machine operator at the plant who had gone missing a few months before.

As the drama unfolded, Mike stood back, careful not to get

in the way of the investigators, no matter how much he wanted to shadow the Sheriff and hear exactly what was said.

CEO Bradley Fletcher arrived with an older man at his side. Fletcher's rosy cheeks turned ashen as he and the older man answered the Sheriff's questions. He walked the pair closer to the pond. When they saw the body, the older man's face twisted in despair and he let out a low wail.

One of the deputies came close enough, and Mike called out quietly, "Any ideas what might've happened?

"Off the record, but looks like a tragic accident. The shop foreman over with Mr. Fletcher said the deceased worked with heavy machinery. Probably his sleeve got caught and got dragged inside. Machines forced him through with the rest of the chemicals and debris, and he got pushed out with the biodegradable scrap." The cop shook his head and walked away.

But Mike wasn't so sure this was a tragic accident. Why had no one heard Bartow's screams? Or noticed that he hadn't left work that day? His wife had surely called the factory. Didn't anybody check?

Pulling his phone from his pocket, Mike shot off a quick text to Madsen asking for background research about carpet mill machinery. He wasn't familiar with the manufacturing process, but he didn't remember reading anything about job fatalities while he was doing his research.

While no one seemed to be watching him, he snapped a few pictures of the body and the responders. Just as the coroner's marked SUV arrived, a beaten down station wagon pulled in front of the SUV. The station wagon skidded onto the dirt and screeched to a halt.

"Shit," Bradley Fletcher muttered loud enough for Mike to hear.

The older man's face fell. Tears that had finally ceased rolled again as he stepped toward the woman exiting the station wagon. Cathy Bartow.

"Tell me, Larry. Just tell me!" She cried, panting, her eyes wild. She wore pajamas, and her hair sprang free of its messy ponytail.

"Cathy, I'm so sorry," the old man said, pulling her into his arms.

She caved against him and wailed as two police officers walked toward them.

"Mrs. Bartow, I'm so sorry. You don't want to see him like this," one officer soothed, urging the pair of them back toward her car.

"I do, though," she snarled as she pulled away from the man she'd called Larry and wheeled around to face Bradley Fletcher. "I need to see...I want to see exactly what you did to him."

The harsh edge in her voice dissolved into racking, heaving sobs and Mike watched as Fletcher stood stock still, his face impassive.

The officer ushered Mrs. Bartow back to her car, and Mike watched as a deputy settled into the driver's seat to take her home. Mike might have snapped a few quick photos of the station wagon and its license plate, but he already knew where Cathy Bartow lived.

CHAPTER FIVE

MIKE WAITED UNTIL THE next afternoon. He walked up the
pathway toward the door, contemplating with every step whether
or not he should turn back. But Madsen had told him to
interview the widow. Try to find any angle other than an
accident to explain her husband's death. Otherwise, he'd been
ordered to pack up and clear out. Chuck Bartow's death was a
police matter now, and Mike had found no hard evidence of any
wrongdoing by Fletcher Textiles.

He hated this part of the job. Imposing on grieving people.
He always felt like a jackal feasting off the carcasses left in
tragedy's wake.

Chuck Bartow may have died because of whatever Fletcher
Textiles was trying to cover up. It was Mike's job to find out,
one way or another. He stepped over a broken bottle and onto the
front stoop of the ramshackle old house.

Before he had a chance to knock, the wind pulled the storm
door out of his hand. It swung open and crashed against the
crackling gray house paint, sending a shower of dry paint
exploding into the air like a puff of smoke.

A low, female voice called out, "Coming."

He wrestled the storm door into place and waited.

When Cathy Bartow stepped into view, her tear-ravaged face a testament to her grief, he wished he'd thought to bring something. Flowers or a card. Instead, all he had was a half-baked conspiracy theory that would send her world into yet another tailspin.

Real nice, Caldwell.

"Look, I can't afford to buy nothing right now, mister, so—"

"I'm not here to sell you anything, Mrs. Bartow. You remember me? We met yesterday at Annalisa Fantz's house? Mike Caldwell. I'm so sorry for your loss." She dropped her gaze to the floor. "I was the one who, uh, discovered your husband's body and I wanted to talk to you about Chuck."

She drew back and flicked a look over his shoulder, glancing up and down the empty street. She seemed too emotionally drained to bother arguing and waved him in with a defeated sigh. "Come out of the chill for a few minutes, then."

She led him to a small dining room littered with empty envelopes and pink paper slips. He'd been broke enough after college to recognize the past-due notices. Lots of them.

Perched on the very top of the pile, sat a slick looking business card that stood out because of its sheer opulence in comparison to everything else in the shoddy little house. The embossed, black letters outlined in gold leaf spelled out Bradley S. Fletcher. CEO of Fletcher Textiles.

Fletcher had paid Mrs. Bartow a visit recently. Strange, after the reception she'd given him at the factory yesterday. The hairs on the back of Mike's neck rose as she gestured for him to have a seat.

"Coffee or something?" she asked, almost reflexively.

He shook his head, and she sat across from him, slumping in her chair like she was a marionette and someone had just cut her strings. "Look, I don't know why you're here, but I got a funeral to plan and—"

"Maaa!" A child's voice bellowed, and her eyes snapped shut like she'd reached the end of her rope.

"I'll be there in five minutes!" She took a moment to collect herself and then opened her eyes. "That's my son, Charlie. He's three. Now his daddy's gone and—" Her voice broke, and she sucked back a sob. "I don't know what I'm going to do without Chuck."

She stared at a spot over Mike's shoulder as she collected herself. Then, sitting straighter, she held up both hands. "State your business so I can tend to my son, Mister…"

"Mike Caldwell," he said again, wishing he were anywhere but here, watching this woman's private hell. "I don't want to make things harder for you, ma'am, you've clearly suffered enough." He leaned in to meet her gaze. "But I'm worried that your husband's death wasn't an accident. Did Chuck ever talk to you about the rumors? Did he believe Fletcher Textiles was dumping toxic chemicals?"

She drummed her knobby fingers on the table as she considered his question for a long moment, keeping her eyes locked on a plate of mostly uneaten toast between them. "Everybody was talking about it a few years back."

"Maaa!"

Her son's screams sent her gaze behind her. "I'm sorry. I'm going to have to—"

He had precious little time. Beating around the bush wasn't an option. "Is that why you moved away from Peru?"

"Partly." She stared at him, nodding slowly. "Houses are

cheaper in Peru, so we had to downsize when we came here. But the schools are better, so…" she trailed off, but her fingers were tap-tap-tapping against her jeans, and he could tell he'd struck a nerve. "Seemed like the safest bet just in case. Mr. Fletcher hired a whole bunch of scientists to make sure those rumors were not true. I was upset out there at the factory. I said some things I shouldn't have."

He'd hired scientists. Scientists kept records. "What kind of things shouldn't you have said?"

She shot a glance to the purse that was sitting next to the stack of bills and then shrugged. "Just looking for someone to blame, is all."

She wet her lips and looked away again.

His instincts were blaring a red alert, but he knew desperation when he saw it. He had to tread lightly. "Mrs. Bartow, you know Annalisa Fantz and her son Dale."

She nodded slowly, pity and guilt written all over her face.

"We were neighbors. In Peru. I was in school with her younger sister."

Mike pressed on. "Annalisa believes that Dale's condition is due to toxic dumping by Fletcher."

The long silence that stretched between them was broken by another wail from the bedroom. "Maaa!"

Cathy's tension ratcheted up a notch, and her eyes went wild. "Look, I'm sure you feel like you're doing the right thing here. But families rely on Fletcher to put a roof over their heads and food on their tables. Rumors—"

He was losing her. He could feel it. So he made a choice. Took a risk. "But they're not rumors, are they? Your husband knew the truth, and that's why he's dead now. So help me, Cathy." He reached for her hand. "Let's get justice for your husband."

Her fingers were cold and clammy, and she gripped his hand as if he was her only lifeline.

"Fifty-thousand," she whispered miserably. She reached for her purse and pulled out a check, laying it on the table between them. "Fletcher gave me fifty thousand dollars for a down payment on a new house in another state."

Mike nodded, afraid to break the spell.

"I said yes because I have a son to take care of. But what Fletcher's doing isn't right." Her voice was flat with a sadness that went too deep for tears. "Not right at all."

Mike stared at the check with all those zeros and that elegant, lilting signature that fairly oozed money, and felt a fierce stab of pity for the widow. A terrible spot to be in. Almost untenable...which was exactly what that bastard Fletcher had counted on.

"If we can prove that Fletcher is dumping toxic chemicals that are contaminating the town water supply—you and I together—you're due far more, ma'am. I know it's asking a lot, but I'd like you to consider sharing your story with EBC viewers. You can cash that check, and I won't tell another soul anything until I can back it up with solid proof." He squeezed her hand and urged her to meet his gaze. "I'm asking you to trust me here. Can you do that?"

His fiancé always said he had a kind face. A face that made old ladies at the grocery store comfortable and drew children to him at the park. He only hoped Cathy Bartow could trust him. He wouldn't let her down.

His pulse hammered as she nodded, sitting straighter in her chair.

"Okay. Okay, let's do it. He had the nerve to roll up here in a fancy Bentley, would you believe? That car cost more than he wants to pay me for my husband's life!" Cathy straightened her spine. For the first time since Mike had arrived, she didn't look quite so defeated. "Fletcher doesn't care about Charlie or me. He didn't care about Chuck or Annalisa or Dale, either. Or any of the other people who live here. All he cares about is lining his pockets."

Mike said a silent prayer as he asked the question he'd been holding back since he walked in. "Did your husband know exactly what Fletcher is dumping and where?"

"He knew it all." She sounded stronger and fiercer by the second. "He wanted to go to the press or the police but he felt like he didn't have enough proof yet. He was afraid he'd get fired trying to get evidence that would make anyone listen. But I know where the proof is. We'll go get it together. Let me put on a pot of coffee and get Charlie to sleep. You can read Chuck's notes until I get back."

Mike nodded. Finally, something solid. Partial proof and a solid motive for murder. Chuck Bartow had died before he had a chance to be a whistleblower, but his wife would close that gap.

CHAPTER SIX

MIKE STOOD WITH CATHY Bartow beside the now-mostly-empty pond where her husband's body had been found. The midnight hour and night-vision goggles that gave everything an eerie yellow pallor contributed to the overall creepy factor. A full onset of gooseflesh all over his body had erupted the moment they'd pulled up to the place and got worse when Cathy used her husband's key to unlock the padlock on the new fence.

He couldn't believe he was actually trespassing at Fletcher Textiles again. Judge Willa Carson would most definitely not approve.

But Cathy had Chuck's keys, and she'd surely have made good on her threat to come here without him if he'd refused to help her. He'd argued until he could argue no more, and Cathy won.

She'd said Chuck was afraid to go to Sheriff Danbury because he was too close to Bradley Fletcher. They were friends. Played poker together once a week. Danbury would give Fletcher plenty of warning. He'd get rid of the evidence, and then no proof would ever exist.

When he thought back to the day before when Fletcher had pulled up, he remembered how quickly the Sheriff went over to talk to him, the length of their chat, and how close together their heads had been during the course of it. At the time, Mike couldn't reconcile their behavior, but it supported Cathy's theory.

Could be Cathy was just paranoid. Or, could be her husband had been murdered, Fletcher paid her hush money and expected her to cover up the crimes. She had good reason to be paranoid.

In the end, the best he could do was extract her promise to get into the plant, gather the evidence Chuck said was stored there, and get out as quickly as possible. And he certainly couldn't let her go in alone.

She tapped him on the shoulder and motioned to keep moving. She knew the layout of the factory and the grounds because she'd also worked here until her son was born. He slung his backpack higher and followed her around the pond, crossing the barren lot toward the back entrance of the main building.

Chuck's notes said that there was a hidden room beyond the boiler room in the basement where the noxious chemicals were kept. He had discovered the room containing unmarked barrels about six months before his death. The barrels were covered with warning labels. He had been afraid to open any of them to get a sample because the concentrated contents and fumes were fatally toxic.

Chuck had taken pictures of the barrels and their labels using a vintage Polaroid camera, which might have been enough to get a search warrant. But Cathy refused to wait. Mike had those pictures on him now, and his backpack contained gas masks and other safety equipment along with collection vials for the samples.

A branch crackled behind him and he wheeled around with a start.

"Who's there?" he demanded, his heart galloping.

Cathy gasped.

He watched a skinny possum scurrying away. He turned to Cathy and shrugged. She continued toward the building. Mike trained his gaze on the building again as they crept closer.

No floodlights blasted on, no sirens blared. Cathy had said that even at the height of the dumping rumors a couple of years ago, Fletcher's security was lax. Maybe because Fletcher had the local cops on the payroll. Or all of the evidence was already destroyed.

Or maybe Chuck had been wrong.

Cathy said there had to be damning evidence inside that building or Chuck would still be alive. She was sure of it, and Mike wanted to believe her. For both their sakes. Otherwise, they'd be in jail before the night was through. He refused to think about what Judge Carson or Lydia would have to say if he got arrested for this.

Cathy reached the side door. The single window pane had been broken and temporarily covered over with a piece of plywood. She reached into her pocket and pulled out Chuck's set of keys. She'd just inserted the right key into the deadbolt when another branch crackled behind them. Mike turned, prepared to curse out their foolhardy little marsupial friend, but before the words left his mouth, a bright light flashed in a shower of red, blinding him behind his goggles.

Pain exploded in his temple, and his vision went black.

He became aware of a steady throbbing, like a stomach-churning drumbeat in his head. He was no longer outside but seated on a cold concrete floor. He fought through the pounding pain and forced his eyes open a crack.

Instantly, a wave of nausea hit him hard enough to make his stomach heave. He closed his eyes again and raised his fingers to touch his temple, gingerly.

"Couldn't leave well enough alone, could you?"

He sheltered his eyes with his hand and blinked, trying to clear his vision, as two blurry figures stepped into sight. He blinked again, and the two slowly became one.

Larry Sumner. The Fletcher Textiles shop foreman. Mike had found his picture online after he showed up at the pond when Chuck's body was found.

The old man swiped at his sweat-dotted brow with the back of his arm as he stepped closer. Now that Mike could see his face more clearly, he realized the man was crying. What the hell was going on here?

As he tried to make sense of it all, the pain in his head was joined by a wrenching ache in his shoulder, and he shifted to ease it but stopped short. He was tied. Trussed up like a game hen and leaning against a massive, metal post in a small room of the warehouse.

"You can't get away, Caldwell." The genuine regret on the old man's lined face was enough to squeeze pain out of the way and make plenty of room for icy terror as clarity returned. "I wish we could let you go, but things have gone too far for that now."

"Is Fletcher making you do this, Larry?" Mike asked, tugging to free his hands from the cord that bound him to the post. "You can still save yourself. I can help you."

"You can't talk me out of it, son. I'm in too deep." The old man blew out a sigh and stared off into the distance.

Mike struggled against his bindings. He wasn't chained. It felt more like a nubby kind of fabric, but Sumner knew how to tie a solid knot.

Just keep him talking. Buy some time to think.

"I can't believe you would kill Chuck in cold blood, Larry. Please...if I'm not getting out of here alive, I need to know the truth. It's the least you can do." Mike held his breath and waited.

"Do you come from a small town?" Sumner asked, finally.

Mike swallowed the knot in his throat and shook his head, ignoring the white-hot pain that blazed through him every time his head moved. "No, sir."

"See, the Fletcher plant here is all we got anymore. All the other places closed up. We have a few local stores, but Fletcher employs eighty percent of the able-bodied people, now that the farms are all gone. No Fletcher, no paychecks." He raked an agitated hand through his thin gray hair. He shook his head slowly.

Another blurry figure walked into Mike's field of vision. He blinked. Twice. "Cathy?"

"Sorry, Mike." Cathy Bartow stood five feet away, holding a pistol aimed at his chest. "When a bunch of city lawyers came sniffing around last year, talking about a few sick kids and chemicals, Fletcher had already cleaned up his act. Stopped the dumping. Got rid of the chemicals. But Chuck wouldn't let it go. Annalisa is my sister-in-law. Did you know that? And what happened to his nephew just ate Chuck up inside."

"That's right. Mr. Fletcher didn't have nothing to do with this. This is a hundred percent on Chuck." Sumner started pacing, mopping at his brow with his shirtsleeve again despite the chill in the air. "It will take some years before the water and soil gets right again, but things are on the mend. Chuck had to go snooping around, digging all this up again, flapping his gums all over town."

Cathy shook her head in mock despair. "It's a shame, is all."

The fabric around Mike's wrists finally seemed to give a bit, and he tugged frantically while trying to keep his voice even and steady. "Is that why you killed him in cold blood, Larry?"

"Of course not." Sumner drew back, stung by the accusation. "No. I caught him same as I caught you. Red-handed. Then I called Cathy."

Cathy grimaced. "You should have weighted him down better, Larry."

"Yeah. He wouldn't stay sunk. I'll do better this time."

Mike expected Cathy to shoot him then, but she didn't. Sumner moved toward a door to the far right, barely visible in the dim light.

Mike craned his neck, straining to see what Sumner was doing in his periphery. He heard the crackle of electricity and an engine chugging to life.

"What is that?" he asked, dread forming a snowball in his belly.

Sumner continued fiddling with something a few feet away. When coils on the wall began to glow a soft amber, Mike gave up trying to stay calm and started struggling in earnest, yanking his hands hard as he rocked forward, desperate to get free. What the hell was this room?

"Cathy, please don't do this." Mike leaned toward her. "You want to protect Peru, keep Fletcher Textiles alive. This isn't the way to do it. The mill will not survive news of two bodies found on the premises in two weeks. You have nothing to gain and everything to lose."

The coils that covered the walls glowed hotter and the chill in the room had already begun to dissipate. Understanding dawned. This wasn't a room. It was some sort of incinerator. The entire room was designed to burn every bit of its contents to ashes.

"Not really a problem. There won't be anything of you to find, Mike," Cathy said as Sumner pushed open a hatch-style door. She backed through the hatch out of the incinerator and squatted, keeping the pistol pointed at Mike. "I'd rather not shoot you first. They might find the bullet."

"Let me knock him out again. It's the humane thing to do." Sumner ambled over to Mike and picked up a blackened brick from the floor.

This was his last chance. His head still weighed a thousand pounds and nausea still coated his belly, but he couldn't just give up. No way was his life going to end like this. Lydia deserved better.

Sumner lifted his brick to knock Mike out.

Mike gave one last, hard tug and the fabric handcuffs broke.

He fell to one side as Sumner's brick descended.

The brick landed hard and solid on his shoulder.

He let out a roar as he struggled to his feet.

He was too weak. He lost his balance. He stumbled.

Sumner was old, but he was strong. He used that split second to send an uppercut straight to Mike's jaw.

Pain screamed through him, but he managed to remain on his feet.

He weaved sideways and blocked Larry's path with his body. Sumner pushed him. Mike had been a wrestler in high school, but that was a long time ago. He remembered the moves. Could he still execute them?

He reached out and wrapped his arms around the man's torso

202 | DIANE CAPRI

and tried to bring him down. The pain in his head and his shoulder would not quit.

He saw Cathy, still outside the incinerator, aim still steady. But the two men were knotted together in a grotesque dance. She didn't have a clean shot.

"Come on, Larry! Let's go!"

"Go on! I'll catch up!" Sumner shouted back.

Cathy shoved the gun into her waistband and ran.

In an instant, Sumner shoved Mike hard to the side. Mike, still too unsteady, stumbled off balance. He let go of Sumner's body rather than fall on the concrete.

The air inside the incinerator was hot and getting hotter. Sweat ran down Mike's face.

Sumner hustled toward the hatch and darted out.

Mike followed, weaving on his feet like a drunken sailor.

Just as Sumner shoved the hatch to close it, Mike pushed his arm through the opening and clutched Sumner's ankle on the other side.

Sumner fell onto the ground floor on the other side and slammed the rusty hatch on Mike's arm. "Let go!"

Mike hung on.

Sumner slammed the door again and again.

Mike bellowed with agony. His arm was surely broken, but he wouldn't let go. With his last ounce of fading strength, he yanked hard on Sumner's ankle and jerked him off balance.

Sumner let out a cry as his leg flew out from under him. He toppled to the ground in a heap. Mike heard a sickening crack when Sumner's head hit the ground and the older man went suddenly silent.

Stars exploded behind Mike's eyelids as he tried to maintain consciousness. He had to get out of here. The incinerator's heat was well over a hundred degrees and fast becoming unbearable.

Mike let his right arm hang uselessly at his side and used his left to pull himself up through the hatch door. He slammed the hatch closed and collapsed on the ground next to Sumner's unconscious body.

Mike's legs quaked as he reached into his pocket and pulled out his cell phone.

The last thing he had heard before he blacked out again was, "9-1-1, please state the nature of your emergency."

CHAPTER SEVEN

THE FLETCHER TEXTILES CRIMINAL dumping scandal had
garnered so much bad press in North Florida that the criminal
case had been transferred to Tampa. Two months after he'd
nearly been cremated alive, Mike sat in Judge Willa Carson's
courtroom as Bradley Fletcher was arraigned on twenty-six
counts of criminal misconduct.

Cathy Bartow was already in jail in Jacksonville, awaiting
trial for the murder of her husband, Chuck. Larry Sumner was in
another cell in the same jail. Mike planned to testify at both
trials. The prosecutors told him all three would be in prison for a
very long time, which was just fine as far as Mike was
concerned.

After the hearing and Bradley Fletcher was led away, Mike
answered Judge Carson's summons to her chambers. Her law
clerk buzzed him through. The Judge was at her desk when he
entered and closed the door behind him.

"Have a seat, Mike," she said, scribbling her name on some
papers. It wasn't an invitation.

He did as he was told.

It took him a few moments to get settled. His right arm was still in a sling because of the injuries Sumner had inflicted to his shoulder. And his left arm was casted for a while longer. The doc said the damage wasn't as bad as it could have been, considering how many times Sumner had slammed his forearm in that heavy hatch door. The headaches had subsided, too. When he was fully recovered, Madsen had promised him the Eyes on Eight gig.

"How are you feeling?" Judge Carson asked.

"Better every day, thanks to Lydia's good nursing care." He nodded as if she needed extra emphasis to believe him.

"I'm glad you're on the mend. I called the judge up in Jacksonville handling Cathy Bartow's case." She paused and cleared her throat. "There's been a development and I didn't want you to hear about it third hand."

Mike sat up a little straighter in his chair. He remembered one of the images of Chuck Bartow he'd used in his Eyes on Eight story about Fletcher Textiles. Bartow was around twenty in the shot, wearing his dress blues popping a salute. Standing adoringly next to him, one hand on his arm, with love gleaming in her eyes was the girl who would become his wife. Obviously, Cathy had adored him back then. What had gone so horribly wrong for those two?

Willa finished signing the orders and laid down her pen. "Cathy Bartow pled guilty this morning on all counts of the indictment. In exchange for testimony against Fletcher and Sumner, she'll receive a life sentence instead of the death penalty."

Mike nodded. He didn't trust himself to speak. And he had no idea what he would say, anyway.

"You achieved some justice for Chuck Bartow." Willa folded both hands on her desk. "Fletcher Textiles was well insured. The civil cases will return some money to the people in Peru. Annalisa Fantz and her son will finally be able to afford the medical care they need. I thought you'd want to know. You did a good thing here." She paused and raised her eyebrows. "And you're damn lucky you didn't die in the process."

"It's too little, too late, though." Mike flexed his fist and then winced. "Chuck Bartow is still gone, and his son without a father. Dale Fantz is still disabled."

"You're right. It's not perfect. Justice rarely is. But you've done all you can for those families. Now it's time to do something for yours." Willa smiled. "Don't you have a wedding to plan?"

THE END

TRUE
JUSTICE

CHAPTER ONE

"HAPPY BIRTHDAY DEAR PAUL, happy birthday to yoooooou!"

The off-key caterwauling of their group had the young law clerk on the receiving end of their song grinning widely, and Ginny Richards grinned right along with him. Paul Brandt was a good egg, and she was honored to call him a friend.

Another law clerk and friend, Mariza Thompson, took point on the cutting of the cake—mocha with espresso chips—as they all chatted quietly, grateful for the break in the middle of the busy day at Tampa's Sam M. Gibbons U.S. Courthouse.

Ginny looked around, warmth spreading through her. This was what she'd hoped to find when she took this job. A sense of camaraderie and belonging that had been missing in her life for so long.

Moving to Tampa had been the second-best decision of her life. Leaving Hank behind in St. Louis had been the first.

Even though she rarely thought of Hank these days, simply remembering his name made her shiver. At first, she'd believed he was her Prince. So attentive. So sweet. Showering her with gifts. Anything she wanted, she only had to mention once, and Hank had made it magically appear.

Then they'd moved into his off-campus apartment together for the last year of law school, and that's when the serious trouble started. His all-consuming jealousy slowly isolated her until she'd had no contact with friends or family at all. At the horrible, frightening end of their relationship, Hank snatched CoCo, her French bulldog, from her arms. He'd bought CoCo, he'd said, and he owned her. Ginny had no choice but to leave her behind.

Escaping Hank had cost her in so many ways that she'd spent months unpacking in therapy, but as she stood back now watching this group of people who had become like a little tribe to her, she felt the rightness of that decision all the way to her bones.

She'd found a home here in Tampa. And she liked it.

"You having some cake?" Mariza asked, nudging Ginny with her elbow.

Ginny smiled and nodded. "Sure, but just a sliver. My stomach is a bit jittery for later."

She'd kept her voice to a murmur, but Mariza ignored the hint. Her violet eyes widened, and she dropped the cake knife with a clatter.

"Holy crap, I almost forgot!" Mariza clapped with glee and cupped her hands around her crimson-lined mouth like a megaphone. "Attention, attention! Everyone, I have an important announcement to make."

Ginny's face burned as she made a grab for Mariza's arm. "Oh my god, please don't!"

But there was no stopping her.

The law clerks all swiveled their heads in her direction expectantly.

"Tonight, at seven o'clock, our very own Ginny Richards is going to be making her singing debut at Valentine's Cellar, the jazz club on Seventh Avenue in Ybor City. Come out to see her. And we can all have a drink for Paul's birthday while we're at it. First round's on me!"

The others broke into a chorus of whoops as Ginny squirmed. She'd planned to work out her butterflies during this first real gig before inviting everyone to see her perform next time.

What if she sucked? But the decision was out of her hands now as the others made plans for later that night.

"So, Ginny, are you planning to wear that pantsuit for your performance?" Jeremy teased, his mouth full of cake.

Jeremy Webber was one of the law clerks hired a few months back, at the same time she was. They'd gone through orientation and new lawyer jitters together. She owned pantsuits in several styles and colors and eschewed dresses and skirts altogether. His teasing drew good-natured chuckles from the others.

Ginny managed an embarrassed smile. "Actually, I have a vintage flapper dress..."

One of the other clerks let out a low whistle, "Wow, that's a first. I wouldn't miss it for the world."

Mariza beamed as she handed Ginny her slice of cake.

"Miss what?" A low voice interrupted from the doorway, and Ginny turned to see her boss, Judge Willa Carson, standing there.

"Sorry," she said, sweeping in and flashing a quick smile. "I missed the singing, but I was in the middle of reading a brief for this afternoon's hearing."

The clerks all murmured hello as Judge Carson turned to

Paul. "Happy birthday. I hope I can still snatch a crumb of your cake even though I didn't get a chance to chime in on the song."

"Of course, Judge Carson. This one's got your name written all over it." He picked up the plate with the largest hunk of cake and handed to her.

"I'll need to skip lunch for this, but it will be worth it," she replied, accepting the cake. "Looks scrumptious. So what were you guys talking about when I came in?" She forked up a bite of mousse and sponge and slipped it into her mouth with a hum of pleasure.

"Ginny has a gig tonight. She just started singing with a jazz band, and this is their first show. Over at Valentine's. She's great. You should come." Mariza nodded enthusiastically.

Ginny chewed on her lower lip, feeling pressured. She liked and respected her boss too much. What if she made a total fool of herself on stage?

Willa nodded as she swallowed. "George and I absolutely love jazz music. Valentine's is one of our favorite hangouts. We'd love to come. Ginny," she turned and gave her a smile. "Can you email me the details?"

"Absolutely." Ginny's stomach did a little flip.

"Perfect. Once you're done here, swing by my chambers so we can go over the materials for this hearing, all right?" Willa swept out of the room, and the group began to disperse. Ginny and Mariza stopped by the coffee pot for a refill before separating to go to their own offices.

"See you tonight!" Mariza called as she rounded the corner out of sight.

Ginny took a long pull of coffee from her mug. Yup. Moving here had been the best thing for her, and every day since she'd arrived in Tampa so far had been proof of it. She had friends, and great job, a cool apartment, and after tonight, a new gig moonlighting as a jazz singer.

The past was firmly in the past, and after a few more stable months, her therapist had said, her nagging sense of foreboding about Hank would surely fade.

CHAPTER TWO

JEREMY, PAUL, AND MARIZA showed up—Ginny had thought they would. But the other law clerks had come, too. Even a few of the secretaries and two court reporters were here.

Front and center, sitting expectantly beside her husband George, was none other than The Honorable Judge Wilhelmina Carson.

Ginny swallowed hard, then pulled down the little flapper headband she'd nestled in her hair. Her heart pounded, and her stomach roiled, but as she smoothed her hands down the low-cut twenties style velvet dress, she focused her breathing, using the well-practiced pattern she'd been taught to implement for moments like this.

Four counts in, hold for four counts, then four counts out.

At her shoulder, something nudged her hard, and she turned to find Steven, the band's drummer, heaving a set of stage lights onto the stage.

"Sorry, kiddo." He grinned sheepishly.

She smiled back and wiped her damp palms on her dress.

The sound check had gone off without a hitch. Now, there was nothing to do but get out there and sing.

Steve flipped on the lights and made a few adjustments before sitting behind the drum kit. He picked up a pair of brushes. The band's warm-up noodling as they waited for her cue gave her something else to focus on, and she mentally ran through the set list before joining them on the stage.

She was ready for this. She'd been born ready. She'd met Hank in college when she was singing in a jazz bar very similar to this one. Another thing he'd taken away from her. One more thing about her life that she was taking back.

Once the lights were in her eyes, the thrill of performing—a tingling, wild anticipation—took hold, sending her anxiety skittering off into oblivion.

The soft patter of brushes on the drums slid over her, and the thrum of the bass made her smile involuntarily as the first note poured from her mouth.

Her voice was smooth and clear. In that moment, she knew it would be all right. She was in her element now, every bit as comfortable inside the music as she was with her nose buried in law books.

It wasn't long before the faces in the crowd became one, and her world became the stories she told through song. She swayed through *My Funny Valentine* and sassed through *Making Whoopie*. She shuffled during *All of Me* and shimmied during *The Girl from Ipanema*.

She hit her cues and all the right notes, and, as the last one rang out, applause exploded from the crowd, filling her with pride.

Mariza had been right after all. Nothing to be nervous about. And even better? Her friends and co-workers filling the seats, ordering drinks and whistling and stomping for her had the old club owner grinning from ear to ear. The band was sure to be invited back again soon.

Mariza faced the group, executed a neat bow and swept an arm back toward Ginny, sending the small crowd into another wave of cheers.

Perfect.

In a word, so far, this night had been perfect.

Ginny risked a glance at the center table to see Willa rising to her feet, eyes full of pride as she clapped furiously while George grinned alongside her. When Ginny made eye contact with Sara, Jeremy, and Paul, they each gave her thumbs up and, with one last bow, she swept from the stage with an overwhelming flood of relief.

After high fives backstage with the band for packing the place, she joined her co-workers in the bar. A jewel-toned Manhattan with a perfect icy film over the top was waiting for her, and she scooped it up with a grateful smile.

"Thank you to whomever is responsible for this drink," she said, holding it up high before taking a refreshing sip.

"You were amazing," Mariza gushed. She already had two empty glasses in front of her, a third well underway in her hand, but Jeremy's praise was what had her blushing.

"You really were, Ginny. You should quit law altogether. That voice," he murmured, shaking his head in awe. "Just amazing."

"We can't wait to hear you again. When is your next gig?" Mariza asked.

Before Ginny could get the words out, two more of her co-workers rushed over.

"The music was great, but I'm more impressed with that

dress." Wendy, one of the older legal secretaries said, letting out a low whistle.

Heat rushed to Ginny's face.

"The dress is smashing, but your pantsuits look great, too," Paul added with a smile.

"Thanks, Paul. And happy birthday again!"

She'd done a short rendition of the birthday song for him on stage, but now she also ordered a drink for him from the bartender with a wave. After all, if it hadn't been for his birthday today, Mariza probably wouldn't have even remembered about her gig in time to tell everyone, so she owed him one.

"What a marvelous performance." Willa's warm voice settled over Ginny, and she turned to see her boss and handsome husband standing a few feet away.

"So impressive. Top notch. We truly enjoyed ourselves. And this place," Willa's husband George gestured around the club, "It's incredible, isn't it?"

Ginny had to agree. Valentine's Cellar was actually underground in a rare, Florida basement room, the place itself was a blast from the past. The dim, red glass candle sconces on every table enhanced the vintage effect.

Ginny grinned. "This was an original speakeasy, you know. Bootleggers and flappers would meet here and cause mayhem. You can almost feel the crime in the air."

"Fabulous." George smiled.

"And you were fabulous." Willa laid a hand on Ginny's shoulder. She paused, scanning the now reserved faces in their small group, and then her smile softened. "But, I think I'm going to leave the rest of the fun to you and your friends. George and I have had enough excitement for one evening. I have case files to review tonight. I'm sure you understand."

"Oh, but—" Ginny started, but Willa waved her off, signaling the bartender.

"Next round's on us," she said, and George set a crisp hundred-dollar bill on the bar.

The cheers rose as one, none louder than Mariza's.

Willa eyed them each in turn, with a stern look rendered ineffective by her smile. "Have a great time, but don't forget tomorrow is a work day."

Willa hooked her arm through George's, and they walked away, but as she passed, Ginny saw her smile and nod. Judge Carson had something of a reputation in the courthouse for being uncontrollable, although most of that came from the Chief Judge's office and everyone knew what a stiff character he was.

The next band began to set up, and Ginny moved to speak with them and with her fellow band mates. When she returned, more of her coworkers stood in a clump at the corner of the bar.

Singing in public was a big step. She'd made the leap from just a couple of work friends to broadening her horizons. Still, despite the night's success, she found herself counting to four, holding for four, and then breathing out for four again before rejoining the group. Her anxiety was under control, but still there. Her therapist had said her underlying condition would probably never go away. But Ginny was determined to kick the worry habit.

Everyone had something to say about which number they liked best, how great the place was, how terrific she looked, and it seemed like the round of drinks the Carsons bought was drained and forgotten in a matter of minutes.

"Feeling overwhelmed?" The voice at her shoulder was so quiet that no one else could hear it, but when she turned to see

Jeremy gazing down at her, she gave him a grateful little nod, glad to know someone understood.

"Yeah, a bit. I do like people, but I'm an introvert at heart, so the stress before I go on stage takes a lot out of me."

"Once you're up there, though…" He shook his head and gave her a half smile. "You're a braver soul than me. So it's my turn to buy the star a drink. Come on, Gin."

He led her by the elbow until they were slightly away from the crowd, then he ordered her a Manhattan.

"You didn't have to do that," she said.

Jeremy rolled his eyes. "It's what friends do when they celebrate."

The bartender plunked their drinks down in front of them, but Ginny didn't take hers right away. Instead, she peered around the crowd again, a strange feeling settling over her. Valentine's wasn't packed full enough to make her feel claustrophobic, but she couldn't deny a sense of tension knotting in her belly and spreading through her limbs.

She let her gaze skim over the faces as she took a sip of her drink, all the while chiding herself. Everyone chatted in muted tones as the band began to play softly in the background.

Which was when she saw him.

He sat in a shadowy corner, his face partly obscured by darkness. She could make out his strong chin and prominent brow. She felt the weight of his stare.

It wasn't Hank. It couldn't be. Hank was still in St. Louis, last she knew. But Hank had been stalking her back in St. Louis, and the stranger gave off the same vibe. He looked enough like Hank that he set her heart to racing and a sense of cold swept over her all at once, like a bucket of ice water had been dumped over her head.

"Anyway, I know this was out of your comfort zone. After everything that happened with your ex—"

"How do you know about that?" Ginny snapped her head back to stare at Jeremy in surprise. She felt like he could read her thoughts. Like he knew she could think of nothing but that man in the corner's eyes boring into her.

"Mariza told me. Sorry, I probably shouldn't have said."

"No, it's fine." She shook her head and then turned to find the man's gaze trained on her, practically unblinking.

In. Two. Three. Four.

Hold. Two. Three. Four.

Out. Two. Three. Four.

But it was no good. Her heart was thundering now, and her glass shook in her trembling hand.

"Look, can I ask a sort of weird favor of you?" she said pausing to take a healthy sip of her drink.

"I'm not going home with Mariza if that's what you're about to ask. She tried last time we were all out together, and I—"

"No," Ginny cut in, shaking her head, "Not that. Could you sort of lean closer to me and pretend like we're flirting?"

Jeremy' surprised laugh bubbled up. "What do you mean?"

"I mean…just come close and pretend for just a second or two. That guy in the corner is giving me the creeps."

Jeremy leaned down to whisper in her ear. "Okay, but you owe me one because Mariza is going to wonder why I told her I don't do office romance and am now cozying up to you."

She leaned up to whisper back, "Okay, consider me in debt. One dumb favor to be repaid at your whim." She pasted a secretive smile on her face as she ran her hand along his bicep and batted her eyelashes up at him. Mariza would understand once she told her what had happened. Mariza knew Ginny sometimes struggled with mild paranoia, too.

"Actually, we should probably get out of here anyway," Jeremy said, leaning down to brush a lock of hair from her face in a fake gesture of tenderness. "The judge wasn't kidding about working tomorrow. We've got an eight o'clock hearing in the morning."

That much was true, and silly or not, the gaze of the stranger had more than killed her performance high. She couldn't wait to get home, change into a comfy pair of PJs and snuggle up behind a locked door.

Which didn't make tonight a failure. Just a slightly less resounding win than it had been ten minutes ago.

Baby steps.

Ginny shot a quick glance to the corner and blew out a sigh when she noted the stranger's seat was now empty.

"Right, yeah. Okay." She nodded shakily.

"I'll even walk you to your car if you're nervous."

She breathed a sigh of relief. "Oh my god, you're a life saver. I know it's silly, but I just—"

"This isn't the best neighborhood in town." Jeremy shook his head. "Better safe than sorry. Say no more."

Their co-workers were onto a new round of drinks and arguing raucously about a case that had just come through the courts, so most barely seemed to notice when she and Jeremy said their goodbyes.

"You good to drive?" Mariza asked, eyeing her blearily.

"Yeah, I didn't even finish my drink. You good to call a taxi when you're done?" Ginny replied with a fond smile.

Mariza held up her phone and shook it. "Already got the address and destination cued up."

Ginny waved to her friend as she and Jeremy stepped into the chilly night. He held out his arm, and she slid hers into the crook as led her out to the parking lot. She knew it was stupid—just a product of her anxiety-addled mind—but every few steps, she took a quick glance around them. Just in case.

When they reached the car, she spun on her heel and thanked Jeremy again. "You're a life saver."

He buffed his nails on his dress shirt and grinned. "I am, aren't I? Now, you go home and get some rest, and be proud of what you did tonight. You were amazing."

She nodded. "Thanks, Jeremy."

"Anytime."

CHAPTER THREE

SLEEP WAS HARD TO get because of her churning thoughts, and she awakened tired and groggy. She had a load of work to get through today before she could collapse into bed to try again tonight.

Ginny showed her valid employee identification and stepped through the metal detector at the courthouse personnel entrance. Unlike members of the general public, who were prohibited from bringing personal electronic devices into the building, her ID exempted her under a standing court order.

"Have you seen Mariza this morning?" she asked Joe Franklin, the U.S. Marshal Service personnel on duty at the security checkpoint.

Franklin shook his head. "Not just yet."

"Can't say I'm shocked. She got in it pretty deep last night."

Franklin laughed. "Yeah, I know. I have seven voicemails to prove it."

"I see." Ginny grinned. "She's probably avoiding you, then."

"I hope not. I already made reservations for our date tonight."

"Good for you." Ginny made her way to the elevator, thinking what she would give to hear Mariza's drunken pleas on Franklin's phone. The messages were likely to be colorful. And explicit.

Ginny would never be as open and forthright, but Mariza's bold choices definitely made her want to stretch out of her comfort zone. She headed straight to Jeremy's office this morning to thank him and tell him that, if it ever happened again, she simply planned to ask the guy why he was staring at her. Could be she looked like his long-lost sister or something. Maybe.

The elevator dinged, the doors slid apart, and Ginny stepped onto the polished marble floors, sweeping past one courtroom after another until she reached the break room. The party must have lasted late into last night because the place was a veritable ghost town. They would all be hurting when they straggled in this morning.

"Poor shmucks." She set up the big coffee pot to brew before grabbing a couple of mugs from the cabinet above. Judge Carson had a full docket today. She'd probably arrived hours ago. She'd be due for another cup by now.

When Ginny arrived at Judge Carson's chambers, she was working behind her desk, door open, reviewing a mile-high stack of papers surrounding her.

Ginny knocked on the varnished wooden doorframe. "Hey. You need a fresh cup?"

Willa jerked her head up, apparently momentarily startled. Then, as she focused in on Ginny, the lines around her eyes and mouth deepened. "Ginny…"

"Sorry. You're busy. I'll just leave this and get to my desk."

"Why don't you come have a seat?" She gestured to one of

the two leather chairs opposite her desk and then shoved aside the papers in front of her.

Ginny walked across the carpet and settled into her seat. Judge Carson looked as if she'd slept very little last night, too. Purple smudges accented her tired eyes.

"Problems with the case?" Ginny asked, her throat getting tighter as the silence stretched between them. "I know you said—"

"No, no. Not that." A grave note had entered the judge's voice, and the familiar coil of dread slithered into a knot in Ginny's stomach.

"You consider Jeremy a close friend, don't you?" she asked.

Ginny furrowed her brow. Jeremy was her equal in the courthouse. They had gone through the new hire process at the same time. She liked him, sure. He was one of her closer friends here, but Ginny was slow to warm up to people. Had someone seen Jeremy pretending to flirt with her and complained?

"We are friends, yes. But if there's some question of impropriety—"

Judge Carson folded her hands on the desk and let out a long breath through her nose. "I'm so sorry, Ginny. I don't mean to be too blunt, but there's no easy way to say this. Last night, Jeremy was found dead in the parking at Valentine's Cellar."

Ginny tried to speak, but breath was knocked from her lungs, and she could only shake her head.

What was Willa even saying? How could that be possible? She'd left Jeremy in the parking lot last night, very much alive. He'd been killed there?

"Tampa P.D. gave me a courtesy call after they positively identified his body because he worked here and witnesses placed me at the club last night. There's no question that the victim was

Jeremy." Willa paused. She cleared her throat. "Don't blame yourself, Ginny. Detectives will want to talk to you, and you should give them your full cooperation. But if you'd like legal counsel, all you need to do is ask. You know that."

"I don't...Jeremy..." Ginny stared at her hands, realizing with a jolt that they were fisted so tightly in her lap that her knuckles had turned white. She shook her head again, desperate to clear it as adrenaline coursed through her in dizzying waves. "How did this happen?"

"Are you sure you want to know all that right now?" Willa asked softly.

Ginny forced herself to meet Willa's gaze. Hiding from the truth wouldn't make it any less true. She steeled herself. "Yes."

"There's no autopsy yet, so we don't know all the facts. According to the preliminary police report, he was attacked from behind, and his throat was cut. Detectives believe he bled to death."

Ginny shook her head, horrified. Kind, sweet Jeremy. All alone in that dark parking lot. How could this be happening?

It didn't make any sense. Jeremy was a friend to everyone. Always helpful. He had no seedy past or dirty family secrets, surely.

Bewildered, Ginny looked up at Willa again. "Was he robbed? Or beaten? I can't—"

Like a flash, the image of the man seated in the corner of the bar last night flickered through her mind, and she recalled the creeping, aching dread that had filled her.

"Listen, Ginny, take the day off. We can manage without you until Monday. The police are conducting interviews at Valentine's this morning. I've been asked for a list of everyone who was there with our group last night. I imagine they'll be making the rounds and asking questions." Judge Carson paused again and cleared her throat. "Maybe one of us saw something that could help, and we don't even know it."

Ginny nodded jerkily, like a puppet moved by an unseen hand. Her whole body felt numb as she left Willa's office. She headed back down the elevator, passing Franklin wordlessly as she rushed by the security station and back to her car.

She sat behind the wheel, motionless, fogging the windows with her tears and rapid breathing. When she finally stopped crying, she slipped the car into reverse and headed home to wait for the police.

As she drove, the deep ache in her stomach crept higher and higher up her throat until she feared she'd have to pull over and retch. And all the while, the image of the man—who looked so much like her ex that he could have been Hank's brother—tortured her mind.

She gripped the wheel tight and spoke to herself sternly. "You were creeped out because he looked like Hank. You're letting your imagination run wild. You need more facts. Maybe Jeremy had an argument over a scratched car door or an altercation with a homeless person."

Even as she said the words, though, she could feel the man's stare—

"Stop!" She slammed her hand against the steering wheel in frustration. "Staring is not a murder weapon. Jeremy wasn't stared to death. Think logically, will you?"

She took a deep breath and thought through the few facts she'd acquired so far.

She and Jeremy had parted in the parking lot. He was headed back inside the club. She drove herself home. Who knew what happened at the club after she left?

She shook her head, grappling again for clarity that was stubbornly refusing to come.

Jeremy.

Poor Jeremy. She'd served as Judge Carson's law clerk for less than a year, but she'd seen so many criminal cases, terrible things that humans did to one another. Yet, it was hard to believe that anyone would want to kill Jeremy at all. Let alone, slit his throat in a dark parking lot. The method seemed overly vicious, somehow.

She pulled into her gated complex and parked in the garage, making doubly sure to lock her car before slogging up the stairs to her apartment. She unlocked her door and, when she was finally safely inside, she threw the deadbolt and fell back against the steel door.

She remembered Jeremy's friendly smile and gentle wit until tears threatened her composure again. She willed herself to stay calm.

Breathe.

In. Two. Three. Four.

Hold. Two—

She choked, resisting the pressure to cry it out, she plopped onto her bed. She was tired, so tired. Sleep. She needed sleep. Eyes still blurred with tears, she bent down to unzip her pointy suede boots when a flash of white caught her eye.

A few feet in front of her on the floor, so close that she'd nearly stepped on it, rested a sealed envelope. Where did that come from? And how long had it been there?

She reached for it, tucked a finger into the tiny opening, and pried the seal open. The ominous *snick* of crackling glue rang through the room. She took a steadying breath as she tugged the letter out and unfolded it. She read it through quickly.

I'm sorry it had to be that way, but I couldn't stand to see you put your hands on him. You won't make that mistake again, will you, Ginny?

After three readings, she comprehended the words. She dropped the letter as if the page had burned her fingers. She fell back on the bed and stared at the ceiling. She wasn't overreacting at all. Her whole body began to vibrate. She felt like Hank was standing in the next room ready to pounce.

She'd read plenty of case files and listened to hours of testimony in cases exactly like this. She knew how this story played out.

She had a stalker.

Stalkers were killers.

CHAPTER FOUR

THE DETECTIVES COULDN'T COME fast enough for her.

Over and over again, she breathed and counted and closed her eyes, but no matter how hard she tried, all she could see were the words on the paper.

This letter had proven beyond a shadow of a doubt the world was a dangerous place. There *was* no safe space anywhere. Jeremy hadn't been safe in the parking lot last night, and she shouldn't have left him there alone.

Your fault. Judge Carson was wrong. You left Jeremy there after he'd gallantly offered to protect you. Jeremy was the one who needed protection.

Guilt mingled with the oozing dread clotting in her veins until she heard a firm knock on her front door.

"Police," a gruff male voice barked, and she rushed to the door to look through the peephole before she opened it.

The man at the door was tall and trim, and the badge on his belt looked extra shiny as if she'd just interrupted him in the act of polishing it.

A cop through and through, to be sure. She hoped he was good at his job.

"I'm Detective Phillip Mason. Homicide."

Relief flooded through her. A detective and two female police officers. "Yes. Please, come in."

Mason said, "You were on our list in connection with the Jeremy Webber murder. You believe the threatening letter and his murder may be connected?"

Ginny nodded. She pointed to the letter she'd dropped on the floor and then sat down with Mason.

"They'll search the premises while we talk, all right? Make sure that whoever left that letter didn't leave anything else behind."

Terror shot through her. "Yes, look as much as you want."

Mason asked a series of perfunctory questions to start.

She fisted her hands at her sides to still the shaking as she gave him her birthdate and a brief work history.

"And how long have you known Jeremy?" he said, pencil poised over the worn notebook he had balanced on his thigh.

"Six, eight months, about?" She crossed her legs at her ankles. As things dragged on, the urge to bolt became harder to suppress. Problem was, she could think of no safe place to hide.

Mason watched her carefully, his keen gaze taking in every movement, which only made it harder to sit still.

"Ginny tell me about yesterday. From the time you first saw Jeremy at work until the last time you saw him. Just cover the waterfront for me."

She stared down at the partially crumpled note inside the evidence bag one of the officers had placed on the table between them. She uncrossed her legs and told her story starting with the conference room birthday cake and moving through the day until she'd left Jeremy, very much alive, in the parking lot at Valentine's Cellar.

"Why did Jeremy walk you to your car?" Mason asked.

She looked down at her lap and cleared her throat. She raised her eyes. "Because there was this guy at the club. He just gave me a creepy feeling. He kept staring at me, and I didn't feel safe, you know?"

"I see." Detective Mason jotted something in his notebook, but from the way his pen moved, it didn't look like much. "Did you know the man?"

She shook her head. Briefly, she considered telling him the man resembled her ex. "He had dark hair. Super short buzz cut, like a military man during basic training, although he seemed too old for that. Late twenties, maybe early thirties. It was dark in the corner. I couldn't see his eyes—"

Mason waited for her to finish and when she said nothing more, he asked, "After Mr. Webber walked you to your car, was there a kiss or an argument, or…?"

She shook her head. "We were just friends. I said I'd see him at work and I left. That was it. But about the guy at the b—"

"We're trying to get a handle on Mr. Webber's interactions during the last hour of his life. This man at the bar, did he have any interaction with Mr. Webber, or anyone else in your group, at any point?"

"I don't think so." She wet her lips and cocked her head to think. "Unless Jeremy went back inside and talked to him after I left. Is there surveillance video? Maybe the man was caught on video?"

"Unfortunately, Valentine's doesn't have any cameras inside or out, they say. We're checking to find other cameras in the area. Maybe we'll get lucky. We'll have DNA results soon." He paused and tapped the evidence bag. "We'll try to match the DNA on this note and its envelope, too."

One of the officers entered the room from behind him. "Take a look at this."

She handed him a box inside an evidence bag. "This was sitting open on Ginny's desk in the bedroom."

The box contained envelopes and note paper, a gift from her mother when Ginny had landed her law clerk job. The envelopes were white but lined in dove gray paper imprinted with intricate gray swirls.

Ginny blinked. "You found that on my desk? I didn't leave it there."

"Where did you leave it?" the detective asked.

Ginny shook her head, "I'm not sure. I've never opened it."

"You've never used the paper or the envelopes?" Detective Mason asked.

Ginny shook her head again.

"These are nice. Custom?" Detective Mason pulled latex gloves from his pocket and opened the envelope. He pulled the box out and examined it on all sides.

"Um, I'm not sure. They were a gift from my mother. She lives in Boston," she replied.

"I've never seen this pattern before. Certainly not common." He opened the box to look at the stationery inside. Then he turned the envelope Ginny had handed him, examining the gray loops and swirls. "We'll confirm, but it looks like whoever wrote this threatening note used your box of stationery."

Ginny blanched. Her hands began to shake again, and she clasped them together to control the trembling. He had been in her house. He'd searched her home to find this box. He'd written the note here, on her stationery.

"Does anyone else have a key to your apartment? Do you have a roommate?"

She couldn't find the breath to reply. She shook her head.

"Ginny," Mason said gently, "Did you write this note yourself?"

She stared at him, so dizzy with the accusation that her vision went black for a second.

"Did you and Jeremy have a fight? Is that what happened? Do you know how common that is? And how uncommon what you're suggesting is? That a stalker you never knew about until today killed a co-worker you're not even sleeping with?"

"The envelope looks bad. I get that. But I didn't kill Jeremy. And I didn't write that note or leave it here. I'll give you whatever forensics you need to rule me out. A lie detector, DNA, my clothes from last night? No need for any warrant or paperwork or a lawyer. It's yours. Just tell me what you want so we can expedite this."

"That's a start." He eyed her long and hard before nodding slowly. "Judge Carson vouched for you. And for what it's worth, I don't think you killed the guy. But if you have anything more to tell me, now is the time to do it."

She stared at him stonily until he inclined his head.

"I'll take those clothes you were wearing last night, then, and call you with a time to come down to the station tomorrow for that polygraph and handwriting sample. Officer Mayes here will take a cheek swab now for DNA, and we'll get out of your hair."

Ginny went to her closet and brought back the dress and shoes she'd been wearing last night. She handed them to the Detective and let them take the cheek swab and then led the three of them to the door.

"If you think of anything else that might help, call me."
Mason handed over a business card, and she took it reluctantly,
thanking him with a half-smile she very much did not feel.

But when she closed the door behind him and double locked
it, she felt anything but safe.

CHAPTER FIVE

TWO HOURS LATER, UNABLE to sleep, Ginny stared at her computer screen. Images of Hank stared back at her. She'd felt compelled to poke through her ex's Facebook page, like sucking on a sore tooth. She was questioning everything at this point. Was it possible that Hank had been at Valentine's Cellar last night? Of course, it was. St. Louis wasn't that far from Tampa. Last night's performance had been advertised online by the band. He might have seen it. He could have found her.

Something about that guy in the bar had instantly triggered her radar. She'd been told she should respect her instincts and snap judgments because they're fast indicators of the truth when her brain hadn't had the time to walk through the evidence. That man *could* have been Hank. But was he?

The possibility had set its hooks into her mind, and she couldn't shake it loose.

As hard as it was to look at Hank in these online photos, knowing that he could have found her, stalked her, and killed Jeremy simply for being close to her when Hank was not—she shuddered.

She flipped through to a fuzzy picture in his collection and leaned in closer to inspect his features. The image was date stamped by the camera two weeks ago. A woman stood with him, near an old barn. Some sort of landmark. The woman looked into the camera, a thin, stiff smile on her lips. She looked haunted, and Ginny felt her heart squeeze in sympathy. Maybe Hank had finally moved on. Maybe he had a new woman, and he'd finally let Ginny go.

Two weeks ago, Hank's hair was still thick and shoulder length. His hair had always been his most prized and distinguishing feature. He had better hair than many women, and he loved to flaunt it. Unless he'd buzzed his off, he couldn't be the strange man who had been watching her at Valentine's Cellar.

She blew out her relief and then laughed aloud. Sure, she was relieved that her stalker wasn't her ex-boyfriend. But she still had a psycho sending her notes, and Jeremy was still dead.

If she were going to survive this, it would help to figure out what had actually happened.

It seemed a nearly impossible task given that it wasn't even five o'clock yet and she was already jumpy and distracted. Lord, she dreaded having to sleep in her apartment alone.

She chewed on the tender flesh inside her cheek, thinking about what to do. She could take a weekend trip to see her parents. Get away from the stalker and give Mason a chance to do his job.

But the thought went as quickly as it had come. When Ginny felt as anxious as this, being with her hovering parents only made the situation worse. She didn't blame them. They'd nearly lost her to Hank, and they were determined not to let her get hurt again. But she didn't want to deal with all of that now, too.

Besides, she'd told Mason she'd come to the police station tomorrow. He'd have more information and more questions. She couldn't help much from Boston.

She finally broke down and popped a Xanax, which she hadn't done in months, but she needed to relax and sleep. Half an hour later, her phone rang. Mariza.

"Hello?" she said, feeling pathetically relieved. She'd gone so long without any real friends. She hadn't thought to reach out to Mariza or the other law clerks. Everyone had liked Jeremy. They'd be upset, too.

"Hey, sweetie. Oh my God, can you believe it?" Mariza's voice was thick with tears, and a loud honking sound echoed through the receiver as she blew her nose. "I can't deal with this alone. Paul called me an hour ago, and we're going to drink through a bottle of wine and just hang. We can bring it over and share if you like."

Ginny squeezed her eyes closed and nodded, forgetting for a moment that Mariza couldn't see her. "That would be great. I'm jumping out of my skin here."

"See you soon," Mariza said, honking again before disconnecting.

Ginny was grateful to have an excuse to tidy up some and focus on something else. By the time Mariza knocked thirty minutes later, Ginny had set out snacks and opened a bottle of wine to share. She peered through the peephole to see Mariza and Paul waving at her.

"We brought food too," she said, hoisting a white plastic bag with Chinese characters on it aloft.

Ginny unbolted the door and swung it open, a trembling smile on her lips. "I'm so glad you guys are here."

Mariza's skin was pale, and her eyes were swollen from

crying, while the whites of Paul's eyes were as bloodshot as a man on a month-long bender.

"Rough day," he said with a grim shake of his head. "I still can't wrap my head around it."

Ginny led them to the kitchen table. They poured wine while she busied herself getting plates and utensils, although they wouldn't be able to eat much.

She set the napkins and utensils on the table with a clatter and, unable to hold it in a second longer, blurted, "I think it's my fault Jeremy is dead."

The tears came again, fast and furious, as Mariza leaped to her feet and pulled Ginny into the circle of her arms. "No, it isn't. You didn't kill him."

Ginny sniffled and shook her head.

"It's a terrible tragedy. You have to see that, or you're going to drive yourself crazy."

When they sat down at the table again, Ginny blew out a long breath and then told them what happened, right down to the threatening letter, watching their faces for dawning judgment. But none came.

"If I hadn't asked Jeremy to flirt with me, he'd still be alive right now," she finished miserably.

Paul's brows were drawn together tight in fury. "I'm sorry you're feeling guilty, Ginny, but the only one to blame is the crazy son of a bitch who's stalking you. You should've called us the second you got that letter. We need to contact those detectives and get them to come back right now and—"

Ginny held up a hand and gave him a watery smile. "I appreciate it, Paul, but I can do that tomorrow. They took the letter and envelope, as well as a cheek swab and my clothes from last night. Tomorrow morning, I'll take the polygraph. I'm confident they'll rule me out in Jeremy's death and help me find the stalker. Until then, I've just got to be careful and alert."

"And not alone," Mariza declared, her wide, blue eyes full of determination. "I can't stay tonight, but I can stay tomorrow night and the next. Paul, can you take turns crashing on Ginny's couch until this is all squared away?"

Paul tipped his head in a clipped nod. "Of course I can. There's no way in hell we're leaving you to deal with this alone while Tampa's finest bumble around."

For the second time that day, Ginny said a silent prayer of thanks. She wouldn't have slept ten minutes here alone, and now, she had not one but two lifelines.

Maybe it was the Xanax and the wine, but she was feeling weepy again, with gratitude this time. She blew her nose. "I can't thank you enough. We'll lock up tight and then drag a dresser in front of the door for tonight. I'll get the locks changed tomorrow."

"No need for that. I've got all the protection we need right here." Paul patted the gun in its holster on his hip, eyes flat with banked anger. "Let the bastard come with another letter tonight. I'll make him regret it."

For the next few hours, they picked at their food and sipped wine as they talked about Jeremy. They started out with pure doom and gloom, but at various points during the night, the apartment rang with laughter at a remembered coffee room joke he'd told or a silly prank he'd played.

By the time they'd polished off both bottles of wine and half the food, Ginny was feeling marginally saner but emotionally and physically drained. Her friends looked as exhausted as she was. Mariza and Paul made plans to switch guard duty the following day at two o'clock, after Ginny's trip to the police station for the polygraph, and Ginny walked Mariza to the door.

"Thanks again. I don't know how to repay you for what you've done tonight. It means the world to me," Ginny said, leaning against the doorjamb.

"It's nothing you wouldn't do for me. This is what friends are for." Mariza leaned in and gave Ginny a hug and then made off down the stairs.

Paul looked on as Ginny locked and then bolted the door. "It's like Fort Knox in here."

Ginny stood back, a hiccup breaking free of her lips. She'd drunk too much wine, but she didn't regret a single sip. Wine and companionship had taken the edge off her fear, and she might actually get a little sleep tonight..

CHAPTER SIX

SLEEP WAS MORE ELUSIVE than Ginny had hoped. She'd tossed and turned for three hours, and the mellow sense of calm from the wine had long since worn off. Now she worried that Paul, stretched out on the couch only a few feet from the front door, was easy prey for the psychopath stalking her.

She already felt guilty enough about Jeremy. She'd never forgive herself if something happened to Paul, too.

She swung her legs over the side of the bed as quietly as she could manage. She'd never appreciated the lack of squeaks and groans in her new apartment more than right now. She didn't want to wake Paul. This senseless crime would forever shadow his birthday. How carefree and clueless they'd all been yesterday morning, joking, laughing and eating birthday cake.

She slid her feet into slippers and crept into the kitchen for a glass of water. She peeked over the back of the couch at Paul's sleeping face and paused to make sure rhythmic breaths lifted his chest.

She went into the kitchen and snagged a bottle of water. She passed by the couch again, shooting a glance at the door to confirm the deadbolt was in place, and she headed toward the bathroom. As she passed her laptop, she frowned. It was open and logged in. She must have forgotten to shut it down.

She ran her thumb over the mouse pad and was about to log off when something made her pause.

Hadn't she been on Hank's Facebook page when Mariza had called?

Now her browser was opened to Google.

She didn't remember closing Facebook. No big deal. She forgot her keys sometimes too.

Still, it was odd because she didn't remember using Google at all.

She tugged the chair out and sat down. She pulled up the browsing history. The first page was her own Facebook profile, which was as far as she got before a deep voice came from behind her.

"Clever girl."

Blood rushed to her ears as she turned to see Paul standing in front of the couch just a few feet away, the strangest smile on his face. "Why would you check your history? No one was here but Mariza and me. Surely you trust us?"

The look on his face became a clown's mask. A horrific mix of pride and rage and love that revolted her stomach. A look she'd seen before. From Hank. The last night before she left him. Right before he'd knocked her senseless. Bile rose up in the back of her throat.

Goosebumps marred her skin as he stepped closer on silent feet. Dear god, she'd invited him into her home and locked them in together. In hindsight, it made perfect sense. Her purse was always lying around at work. He could've swiped her keys on one of any number of days and made a copy to get into her apartment to leave that letter.

She'd welcomed the enemy into her home. Now she had to get him out.

Old habits she'd learned for dealing with Hank's volatility came flooding back. *Act normal. Pretend you don't suspect him.*

"No problem. You can use my computer anytime. Of course, I trust you," she said quickly, forcing a stiff smile. "I thought I turned it off, is all, and couldn't remember why I didn't."

He eyed her steadily. She pushed herself to stand and gripped the edge of the desk. "I-I'm going to go back to bed now, though. Sorry for waking you."

She shuffled toward her room, heart knocking like a trapped bird against her ribs. If she could get through the door and lock it, maybe she'd have time to call 9-1-1 before he broke it down.

But Paul was agile and had a long stride. She'd barely moved three feet before he was on her, looping his arm around her neck and plastering her back roughly against the length of his body.

"I'm not an idiot, Ginny. That's the mistake you keep making. You told us that you weren't into Jeremy, but I saw you—" He broke off with a furious snarl and pressed his mouth against her ear. His whisper was terrifying. "I saw the way you looked at him. And now, I come here to take care of you. To be here when you need me. To prove I can be all that you need so you can stop acting like such a little slut. Only to find out you're looking up pictures of another man on Facebook? Who is he, Ginny? Some guy you screwed? Or some guy you *want* to screw?"

His breath was hot on her cheek and his grip around her neck tightened. She curled her fingers around his forearm and tugged. "Please, it's not like that. He's my ex. I don't want to be with him. I suspected he was the person who killed Jeremy. I swear."

She had to keep her wits about her. Make him think that she wanted him. He might believe her.

"Don't lie to me, Ginny. It's all the lies that drove me to this." Spittle struck the side of her face, and she shuddered. "I'm not sure I can trust you now. You're not the Ginny I fell in love with at all."

She felt the hard length of his pistol digging into her side, and she swallowed. After Hank, she'd taken several self-defense classes. What was she supposed to do now?

Distract and disarm. Distract and disarm.

"I am, though, Paul. I am that Ginny. I made some dumb mistakes. To be fair, though, you never let on that you liked me." She forced a laugh, but it came out a wheeze. "Can you loosen your hold a little? I really want us to be able to talk, but it's hard with your arm pressing on my windpipe."

There was a long pause before his hold relaxed, just slightly. "Talk."

"I thought you were so handsome and smart. If you had just asked, I'd have chosen to be with you in a heartbeat."

She could almost feel his indecision, and she took a gamble, pulling away from his now-unresisting grasp and turning in his arms until they were face to face.

"In fact, why don't you ask me now? Just forget about all of the rest of it, and tell me how you feel."

She garnered every bit of courage she possessed and raised a shaking hand to his cheek to stroke it gently. Lovingly.

His wild eyes went suddenly soft and a little wistful.

"Since the first day I saw you, I knew I wanted you to be mine," he murmured, muscles relaxing as he slid his arms loosely around her waist.

She leaned into him, pressing her ear to his beating heart.

His voice droned on as he talked about love at first sight, but she barely heard him. She was like a child playing a game, waiting for the exact right moment to—

She pulled her leg back and drove her knee into his crotch with every ounce of power she could muster. He howled in pain and shoved her away.

There was no time to call the police. She had to get out, and fast.

She turned, her heart pounding in her ears. She had to get past him somehow and out the front door.

Already, though, he was lunging at her again, his hands outstretched with maniacal anger. She used his height to her advantage, ducking low and letting his momentum throw him off stride.

She sprinted to the door. Her fingers grappled for the lock. Pain screamed through her from head to toe.

Her scalp was on fire as he fisted a hand in her hair and dragged her backward. She cried out, socks slipping on the polished floor. A second wave of pain washed over her and her vision went blurry as she hit the floor, hard.

Almost blind in her desperation, she reached to him, trying to gouge his eyes, to kick at any part of him she could reach, but he pinned her back easily. And then both his hands were on her throat, and she was flailing, trying to pry his fingers from her neck as the world went fuzzy and colorless.

In her periphery…a glint of metal in the moonlight streaming through the window that made her hold on. Her vision tunneled, and her lungs burned as she clawed at Paul's relentless grip with one hand and reached for the glinting object with the other.

Please, God, let that be what I think it is.

She yanked as hard as she could to free his gun from the holster.

A moment later, he realized what she was trying to do.

He squeezed her throat harder.

She pulled the gun free. She had no time to aim.

He squeezed the last bit of oxygen from her throat. "You b—"

But his words were cut off by the sound of the first shot. The second hit him. He knocked her arm away, and the third shot went wide.

Her ears rang, and the acrid scent of gunfire filled her nostrils.

She held his gun in front of her, trained on his chest. His eyes bulged with shock as he released her neck and toppled backward. A wide bloodstain covered his shirt, but she'd hit him above the heart, closer to the collarbone. His blood still pumped, pooling around his body.

Her whole body quaked as she crabbed backward, kicking away from him until she could stand, unencumbered. Gun held straight, as she'd been taught, pointed at his chest.

"Don't move, Paul," she murmured, a slick of nausea rolling over her. "I promise you, if you move, I'll shoot you again, and I'll keep shooting until you're dead."

The truth of her words must have resonated with him because he nodded and stayed put. He raised one hand to his wound, attempting to staunch the bleeding.

She reached across to grab a towel and tossed it to him. "Press that to your wound. Maybe you won't bleed to death before the medics get here."

She backed slowly toward her bedroom, keeping the gun pointed at him as she fumbled for her phone and pressed the redial button.

The operator's voice squawked over the open line. "Nine-one-one, state the nature of your emergency."

"I shot an intruder in my living room. Please send an ambulance immediately."

She flipped on the lights and looked around her apartment. Nothing seemed amiss. No broken glass or furniture to reflect the attack. As far as she could tell, her home looked like it always did.

She heard the sirens in the distance, coming closer. Paul's face was deathly pale, but he still breathed. He might make it if he could hold on a little bit longer.

The sirens preceded the ambulance and the police cars like lightning precedes thunder. But just as surely, the vehicles arrived and screeched to a halt in the parking lot. First responders pounded on the door and barged through until they found her. And him.

After that, everything was a swarm of activity.

Paramedics dealt with Paul quickly and soon had him on a rolling gurney on his way out the door headed for emergency surgery at Tampa Southern Hospital.

She wasn't sure what happened to the gun. If she'd dropped it from her shaking hands or if, more likely, Detective Mason had peeled her hand away from the grip and led her back to the kitchen.

Mason spoke to her sympathetically, and though she didn't listen to the words, she knew he was apologizing. His face had taken on a sickly greenish-gray color. He tried to soothe her, to provoke her into saying "I told you so," to assuage him of his guilt, but all she wanted was for him to leave.

For *all of them* to leave.

A clock ticked in the next room, and she pulled her knees up to her chin, hugging them close to her. She breathed, in for four, hold for four, out for four. And the clock kept ticking, slower and slower each time.

Maybe all of it would feel okay again. Someday.

While they were still milling about her apartment, she glanced at her phone. She blew a deep breath out her nose and then dialed the first person that came to mind.

"Judge Carson? It's Ginny Richards. Listen, I know it's late, but I need a lawyer."

CHAPTER SEVEN

"GIG LATER TONIGHT, RIGHT, Gin?"

Ginny looked up from her Caesar salad to see two of the secretaries standing over her table.

"Yup, eight o'clock."

They both promised to be there and strolled away, chatting among themselves again, leaving Ginny and Mariza to their lunches.

"You going to be all right with this?" Mariza asked, craning her neck until Ginny was forced to look up and meet her probing gaze.

It had been a month since Jeremy's death, and Ginny was still on edge.

Her mental state had been dicey. Judge Carson had insisted that she move into a guest room at their home, Minaret, where both George and Willa could keep an eye on her. She hadn't left the house that first week. Every time she tried, she broke into a cold sweat. Willa's beloved Labrador Retrievers, Harry and Bess, followed Ginny everywhere, which helped. But they were really nothing more that big lap dogs.

She'd wondered if she'd ever be able to perform again or would have to quit the band altogether.

After his surgery, Paul had confessed to everything. Stalking her, Jeremy's murder, breaking into her home. Knowing that he would be behind bars for decades to come had helped Ginny feel a bit braver, more normal.

She still had a life to live. A job to do. Friends to keep. Hard as it was, she couldn't stay in bed and pretend that everything had been a terrible dream. What happened—with Hank, with Jeremy, with Paul—had happened. But there were still things to be grateful for.

Through it all, though, her friends had saved her. Mariza and the other law clerks never wavered. They came each day, checking on her, bringing conversation and caring. Even Willa, who was the busiest person she knew, made time for her when she came home from court in the evenings. And she'd certainly had plenty of great food from George's chefs every night.

The power of those friendships warmed her heart. She still had a long way to go, although she minimized everything when she talked to her parents once a week. Otherwise, they'd have insisted that she come to Boston where they could coddle her forever.

Guilt weighed on her in the dark of night. And if she'd been slow to trust before, she was even more so now. But she'd finally emerged from the darkest part of her grief and fear, and she'd come out the other side bruised, battered, and very much alive.

"Gin?"

Ginny worked up a smile for Mariza and thought about the stage and the music, and seeing her friends rally around her, and she nodded.

"Yeah. Yeah, I think I am. Ready."

THE END

I hope you enjoyed *Justice Is Served* as much as I enjoyed writing it for you. Judge Willa Carson stars in the bestselling Hunt for Justice Series. Read more Judge Willa Carson books to spend some time with Tampa's feisty federal judge. Here's the full list in order of publication:

THE HUNT FOR JUSTICE SERIES:
Due Justice (Judge Willa Carson)
Twisted Justice (Judge Willa Carson)
Secret Justice (Judge Willa Carson)
Wasted Justice (Judge Willa Carson)
Raw Justice
Mistaken Justice
Cold Justice (Judge Willa Carson)
False Justice (Judge Willa Carson)
Fair Justice (Judge Willa Carson)
True Justice (Judge Willa Carson)

I hope you'll recommend my books to your friends who might like them, too. The best way to share your honest review of my books is to post a quick two or three-sentence review where you bought this copy and give the books some stars. Please do that. I promise I won't forget! And now that we've found each other, let's keep in touch. Readers like you are the reason I write!

BOOKS BY DIANE CAPRI

THE HEIR HUNTER SERIES:
Blood Trails
Trace Evidence

THE HUNT FOR JUSTICE SERIES:
Due Justice (Judge Willa Carson)
Twisted Justice (Judge Willa Carson)
Secret Justice (Judge Willa Carson)
Wasted Justice (Judge Willa Carson)
Raw Justice
Mistaken Justice
Cold Justice (Judge Willa Carson)
False Justice (Judge Willa Carson)
Fair Justice (Judge Willa Carson)
True Justice (Judge Willa Carson)

THE HUNT FOR JACK REACHER SERIES:
Don't Know Jack
Get Back Jack
Jack and Joe
Deep Cover Jack
Jack in a Box
Jack and Kill
Jack in the Green
Jack the Reaper

ABOUT THE AUTHOR

Diane Capri is an award-winning *New York Times, USA Today*, and world-wide bestselling author. She writes several series, including the Hunt for Justice, Hunt for Jack Reacher, and Heir Hunter series, and the Jess Kimball Thrillers. She's a recovering lawyer and snowbird who divides her time between Florida and Michigan. An active member of Mystery Writers of America, Author's Guild, International Thriller Writers, Alliance of Independent Authors, and Sisters in Crime, she loves to hear from readers and is hard at work on her next novel.

Please connect with her online:

http://www.DianeCapri.com
Twitter: http://twitter.com/DianeCapri
Facebook: http://www.facebook.com/Diane.Capri1
http://www.facebook.com/DianeCapriBooks

If you would like to be kept up to date with infrequent email including release dates for Diane Capri books, free offers, gifts, and general information for members only, please sign up for our Diane Capri Crowd mailing list. We don't want to leave you out! Sign up here:

http://dianecapri.com/contact/

BONUS
CONTENT

TRAVIS McGEE AND ME*

by Diane Capri

Once upon a time in a galaxy far away, I lived in the land of
the frozen tundra. Which is to say Detroit. Where the weak are
killed and eaten. Where a twenty-six mile commute can take
three hours to get to work and another three to get home. Where
the entire month of February can pass without a single ray of
sunshine. Where no palm tree has gone before or since.

On a particular day in April, 1992, my car was parked in the
southbound expressway's fast travel lane as I was two hours late
for work. Again. A snowstorm had dumped twelve inches of
snow overnight. Traffic moved not at all. Indeed, a co-worker
who traveled the same commute actually turned off his car two
lanes over and joined me to chat awhile. Mostly we talked about
how our plans for the afternoon were, well, snowed under.

What plans? Did I not mention this was opening day of
baseball season?

I'd been offered a great new job in the Sunshine State a few
weeks before. The decision-making process was somewhat
agonizing. Leave Michigan? Leave my job? My friends? My
neighbors? These questions plagued me. Until.

Until my friend returned to his vehicle and I remained in the
car alone and a song came on the radio and answered everything.
You know the song. The Beach Boys. Places in the lyrics. Starts
out, "Aruba, Jamaica, oooooh I wanna take ya…" Right?

There were places in the world where the sun shines almost
every day. Where a lanky boat bum named Travis McGee hangs
out with Meyer. Where gin martinis flow like water and
mysteries are settled with humor and dispatch. Where sand-

warmed beaches flow into warm salt water. Perpetual summer in the land of flowers was looking pretty good to me right about then.

So I decided. Right that second. To live in perpetual summer, write mysteries set in Florida, and if I wanted snow, why from that April onward, I could fly to it.

Of course, I took the job. Practicing law was something I loved then and still do. But I wrote Florida mysteries, too. I wrote about justice primarily. I was following that time-honored advice to write what I knew. And also because our justice system was more about the system and less about the justice, it seemed to me. I wanted more justice, less system back then—and still do.

What followed, so far, were five novels in my Justice Series, featuring lawyers and judges in Florida working inside and outside the system for justice. Solving mysteries, providing a few thrills and quite a bit of suspense along the way. Oh—and the Florida Fantasy, too.

What is the Florida Fantasy? You know it, don't you?

Judge Willa Carson lives not on a houseboat, but her own island nonetheless. She drinks red wine, not gin, and eats gourmet food every day and never gets fat. She's married to her prince, George Carson, who is every bit as agreeable and intelligent as Meyer. George never gets in the way but is always there when Willa needs him, complete with great coffee, love, and understanding (mostly). Beach bunnies are ever so much more trouble for Travis than Willa's two adorable Labradors. Harry and Bess are boon companions who don't chew the furniture or mess up the house. Willa hits a straight, long drive off the tee every time instead of winning at poker. And of course, she drives a vehicle much more attractive than Miss Agnes. Like

Travis, Willa goes her own way and helps others find justice in an unjust world. She's tall, too.

Willa Carson finds herself dispensing *Due Justice*, exposing *Twisted Justice*, uncovering *Secret Justice*, lamenting *Wasted Justice*, observing while Jenny Lane reveals *Raw Justice* and remains unaware of *Mistaken Justice*.

Jess Kimball handles Florida fantasy more realistically when she teams up with Governor Helen Sullivan in a pitched battle against a clever stalker bent on killing them both in *Fatal Distraction*. Jess Kimball, it turns out, can be a *Fatal Enemy*.

Willa Carson, Jenny Lane, and Jess Kimball never succumb to *The Long Blue Goodbye* or *The Lonely Silver Rain* or any colors between. No, tropical drinks and steel drum bands in the Sunshine State are more our speed.

This article originally appeared in Mystery Readers Journal.

WHEN LIFE HANDS YOU LEMONS, MAKE MARTINIS — WITH A TWIST!*

How The Hunt for Jack Reacher Series *Was Born*

by Diane Capri

Life was humming along on all cylinders for a while. Born in Alabama, I grew up in a small German-American farming town north of Detroit, where I lived a book-filled childhood and followed most of the rules. Graduated from Wayne Law School cum laude and served as an editor of the *Wayne Law Review*. Ranked in the top 1% of lawyers nationwide, and practiced law throughout the U.S., representing clients from around the world. While I published millions of words during my legal career, most of them were nonfiction. Never drank gin martinis, shaken or stirred.

Always an insatiable reader with a keen interest in crime fiction, particularly mystery and suspense, I spent the travel years on airplanes and in hotel rooms. I put the time to good use by learning fiction craft when not practicing law, but friends pointed out that my fiction files contained only desire and incomplete projects. Too true. Grisham and Turow and many other lawyers hit the fiction world long before me.

But in 1995, one shocking phone call destroyed my thriving law practice. My largest client was overwhelmed by product liability lawsuits and filed for bankruptcy protection, blasting a gaping hole in my by-the-book life and leaving me with an uncollectable debt besides.

Pelted by these lemons, gin martinis were a viable option. But I don't like gin. I've been called a Pollyanna and perhaps that's true, because I was sure I could find a better answer. Like what? Well, I loved that creation story about the famous author who got fired at age 40 and became Lee Child.

Of course, I hadn't heard that story in 1995 and he wasn't famous then.

I had heard the one from the medical clerk who wrote *A is for Alibi* to kill off her ex-husband and become Sue Grafton. I didn't have an ex-husband, but more than a few folks had recently made my list of jerks the world could do without. Hmmm…

I'd been through Travis McGee's adventures a dozen times, never tiring of exploits that traveled along smoothly on Boodles Gin. I'd moved to Florida and adored everything about the Sunshine State. The hours to write what I loved instead of what paid the bills now stretched endlessly ahead and I figured it was now or never.

So sure, Pollyanna, why not?

You're thinking I acquired a taste for gin martinis, killed off the bad guys, finished the book, and lived happily ever after? Um, not exactly.

After a series of false starts, I challenged myself to finish **Due Justice** in the style of stories I loved to read, put my head down and went to work.

Due Justice and the three books that followed are suspenseful Florida mysteries set in the legal world. Rather than a strapping, muscular boat-bum like McGee, my hero is Federal Judge Wilhelmina Carson, a strong woman who drinks Bombay Sapphire Gin and delivers true justice along with a splash of humor. The Willa books quickly found a publisher, an audience, and acclaim as well, under another author name.

So, not Lee Child or Sue Grafton, but there I was, up and

running, humming along on all cylinders again. All's well that ends well? Not so fast.

You guessed it: Another fusillade of lemons.

Slammed by lawsuits, my publisher failed and bankruptcy followed. A legal quagmire swamped my career. Again. And this time, it swallowed my books, too.

Quick! Juice those lemons! Shaken? Stirred? Who cares? Bring on the martinis and keep 'em coming! Except Pollyanna doesn't like gin, as it turns out. Nor is she a loner.

We all get by with a little help from our friends and writers are some of the most generous people anywhere. I'd long been active in Mystery Writers of America, Sisters in Crime, Romance Writers of America, and other writing organizations. The friends I'd made there encouraged me to get back to work.

While Judge Willa was literally being held hostage, I wrote two new thrillers, one featuring Florida lawyer Jennifer Lane, and the second starring victim's rights advocate Jess Kimball and her good friend, Florida Governor Helen Sullivan. These books featured ramped-up suspense and increased body counts, mostly within the bounds of the law. Sue Grafton was right about literary revenge. Very satisfying. Easier on the liver than gin martinis, too.

While I was writing Fatal Distraction, I was invited to join International Thriller Writers at its inception. Shortly thereafter, I became a member of the ITW board along with my friend, the #1 International Bestselling author, Lee Child.

At a cocktail party in New York in 2009, without a martini in hand, Lee and I discussed one of the great existential questions: Where the hell is Jack Reacher between exploits, anyway?

The answer was unknown, which inspired me to write a series of suspense novels answering the inquiry with Lee's blessing and support. The first of those novels is *Don't Know Jack*, introducing FBI Special Agents Kim Otto and Carlos Gaspar.

Thankfully, readers enjoyed the tale. They made **Don't Know Jack** a bestseller, allowing the single, *Jack in a Box* to quickly follow. All of my books are now enjoying wide readership again, proving there is life after bankruptcy.

I hesitate to tempt fate by saying we're humming along again. Yet, The Hunt for Jack Reacher series is great fun. We travel behind Reacher and discover what happened to the people left behind in his wake. **Jack and Kill**, **Get Jack Back**, and **Jack in the Green** are now available and I'm writing as fast as I can to create more.

Readers ask me whether Otto and Gaspar will find Reacher at some point. My answer is: sure, whenever Reacher wants to be found. Who will win the inevitable confrontation? My money's on Otto. I'll understand if you feel differently. After all, Reacher's bigger, stronger, meaner, and much less anxious. So what? The bigger they are, the harder they fall.

For now, I'm still a snowbird. We live in perpetual summer, dividing our time between homes in Northern Michigan and Florida. Still married to my one and only husband. Still love dogs, writing, sunshine, warm temperatures, gourmet food, red wine, convertible cars and my very large extended family. I never developed a taste for gin.

I'll always love Willa Carson, Jenny Lane, Jess Kimball, and reading Travis McGee. But these days, I'm also busy on The Hunt for Jack Reacher. Want to come along? Bring vodka—life will supply the lemons.

* This article first appeared in Mystery Readers Journal

DIANE CAPRI REVEALS LEE CHILD*

There's no nicer guy on the planet than my friend Lee Child. He's kind, amusing, normal. What's not to like?

You probably feel the same. He's smiling and blue-eyed friendly in all those author photos, right? What we see is what we get with Lee Child.

So I asked him if he wanted to be *revealed* to Licensed to Thrill readers when his latest book was released. I figured we'd have a little fun, be a bit irreverent, maybe share some things about one of the world's most beloved authors you didn't already know.

I wasn't nervous at all at first. That was dumb. Because I forgot one of Kim Otto's first rules: You never see the bullet that gets you.

The first unheeded warning was when Lee sent me his self-portrait before our chat.

As a person who's vertically challenged, I peered up through my binoculars and covered the most important point first.

Diane Capri: Someone recently described you as a lanky praying mantis. How tall are you, anyway? Ever wish you were shorter? I mean, don't you get light-headed at that altitude?

Lee Child: I'm about ten inches tall when I'm lying down. About 6-4 when I'm standing up. Very thin, no matter how much I eat. I like being tall. Who wouldn't? There are many completely unearned advantages. Like having an English accent—in America that's 20 unearned IQ points, right there.

Diane Capri: Readers want to know some personal details about you that Charlie Rose didn't ask. Let's start with a few of those. Here's an easy one. You were chewing gum when I saw you last in NYC and not hanging around the smoking sections. Have you quit smoking?

Lee Child: No, I'll never quit smoking. I enjoy it. It's one of my main pleasures in life. Every New Year I make the same resolution—keep on smoking.

Diane Capri: You know Kim Otto is hunting for Reacher in *Don't Know Jack,* and she's more than a little worried that she might actually find him before she's ready. She worries about Reacher's facility for, um, solving problems. Your fans write, warning me not to disrespect Reacher because he's one of the good guys. Clearly, Jack Reacher's A Wanted Man—in more ways than one. That's got to make you somewhat, well, let's call it pleased. How does all this attention affect your life? Does your wife, Jane, still make you take out the trash and handle the broken toilets like a normal husband?

Lee Child: Oh, sure. I haul trash and fix things like any guy. I'm a qualified electrician, from backstage jobs in the theater. Also a qualified firefighter, for the same reason. Away from the hoopla, I live a completely normal life.

Diane Capri: Um, okay, thanks for sending along that picture of where you live… It fascinates me that your daughter, Ruth, has an amazing facility for languages. Did she inherit that from her parents? How many languages can she speak fluently? And what kind of work does one do with that talent, anyway?

Lee Child: Ruth speaks most of the European languages, and if there's one she doesn't, just wait a day or two until she masters it. It didn't come from me or Jane. From my mother, possibly. Maybe it's one of those things that skips a generation. My mother had a similar talent. Ruth works at NYC's famous Gay and Lesbian Center, dealing with people who don't speak

English so good. She can do sign language too. And sign language for the blind.

Diane Capri: Like most writers, you read widely and love books. It's astonishing that our Florida crime writers' patron saint, Travis McGee, remained undiscovered to you until the mid-1990s, long after John D. McDonald died. Not surprising that you're a fan and McGee has influenced your work, though. When you created Reacher, you avoided duplicating character traits that contemporary crime writers had already developed, but like you and McGee, Reacher is a tall dude. Does Reacher share any of McGee's other traits? Do you?

Lee Child: Not really. McGee was pretty sure of himself. Reacher is professionally, as am I, but personally we're a lot more diffident than old Travis. No grand pronouncements for either of us.

Diane Capri: We're all looking forward to reading *A Wanted Man*, which just opened to raves from readers and critics and at the top of the best seller lists. This is Reacher's 17th chance to get his butt kicked. Is that gonna happen?

Lee Child: He has a busted nose in this one, carried over from the last one. (Well, not the last one, which was a prequel. The one before.) It was a challenge not to write anything about smells. Normally I'm a five-senses-all-the-time writer.

Diane Capri: Many readers have already devoured *A Wanted Man* and wait hungrily for Reacher #18. They want to put the title on their wish lists. What is it?

Lee Child: It's called "Never Go Back"—because Reacher goes back to his old unit HQ and falls into a world of trouble.

Diane Capri: Well, sure. Trouble always finds Reacher. The other thing we're looking forward to is the new film titled simply Jack Reacher, starring Tom Cruise. Cruise fans are swooning already; some Child fans are a bit less ecstatic. You've seen the film and loved it. Why?

Lee Child: It's a fast, hard movie, and Cruise nails it dead on. How? Because he's a great actor. They do that stuff for a living. The rest of the cast is spectacular too. Altogether awesome. Plus it has a better car scene than Bullitt.

Diane Capri: When we put Reacher on trial for murder at the very first ThrillerFest, the still-to-be-revealed Kim Otto took Reacher on, sort of. Otto made darn sure everything went according to the law and Reacher still got off. But only because he cheated. Otto will be smarter next time they meet. Is Reacher worried?

Lee Child: Reacher didn't cheat. It was jury nullification, pure and simple, because of his charm. Sure, he said with a smile, I killed the guy. Not guilty!

Diane Capri: Um, that's a little unnerving, actually. For the first time ever, you're headed to my summer town. I feel a bit like Kim Otto. She knows Reacher is watching her, and it's a little creepy and she's not all that thrilled about it. Of course, I'm looking forward to seeing you, but what brings you to Northern Michigan? Tell me straight. Are you stalking me?

Lee Child: Yes. Fortunately for me there's a great author event there, for cover. Be afraid.

He said that with a smile.

*This interview appears in color and with photographs on Diane Capri's website at www.dianecapri.com.

THE REACHER REPORT:
March 2nd, 2012

...THE OTHER BIG NEWS is Diane Capri—a friend of mine—wrote a book revisiting the events of KILLING FLOOR in Margrave, Georgia. She imagines an FBI team tasked to trace Reacher's current-day whereabouts. They begin by interviewing people who knew him—starting out with Roscoe and Finlay. Check out this review: "Oh heck yes! I am in love with this book. I'm a huge Jack Reacher fan. If you don't know Jack (pun intended!) then get thee to the bookstore/wherever you buy your fix and pick up one of the many Jack Reacher books by Lee Child. Heck, pick up all of them. In particular, read Killing Floor. Then come back and read Don't Know Jack. This story picks up the other from the point of view of Kim and Gaspar, FBI agents assigned to build a file on Jack Reacher. The problem is, as anyone who knows Reacher can attest, he lives completely off the grid. No cell phone, no house, no car...he's not tied down. A pretty daunting task, then, wouldn't you say?

First lines: "Just the facts. And not many of them, either. Jack Reacher's file was too stale and too thin to be credible. No human could be as invisible as Reacher appeared to be, whether he was currently above the ground or under it. Either the file had been sanitized, or Reacher was the most off-the-grid paranoid Kim Otto had ever heard of." Right away, I'm sensing who Kim Otto is and I'm delighted that I know something she doesn't. You see, I DO know Jack. And I know he's not paranoid. Not really. I know why he lives as he does, and I know what kind of man he is. I loved having that over Kim and Gaspar. If you haven't read any Reacher novels, then this will feel like a good, solid story in its own right. If you have...oh if you have, then you, too, will feel like you have a one-up on the FBI. It's a fun feeling!

"Kim and Gaspar are sent to Margrave by a mysterious boss who reminds me of Charlie, in Charlie's Angels. You never see him...you hear him. He never gives them all the facts. So they are left with a big pile of nothing. They end up embroiled in a murder case that seems connected to Reacher somehow, but they can't see how. Suffice to say the efforts to find the murderer, and Reacher, and not lose their own heads in the process, makes for an entertaining read.

"I love the way the author handled the entire story. The pacing is dead on (ok another pun intended), the story is full of twists and turns like a Reacher novel would be, but it's another viewpoint of a Reacher story. It's an outside-in approach to Reacher.

"You might be asking, do they find him? Do they finally meet the infamous Jack Reacher?

"Go...read...now...find out!"

Sounds great, right? It's available. Check it out and let me know what you think.

So that's it for now ... again, thanks for reading THE AFFAIR, and I hope you'll like A WANTED MAN just as much in September.

Lee Child

Printed in Great Britain
by Amazon